# NIVES

Sacha Naspini

# NIVES

*Translated from the Italian
by Clarissa Botsford*

Europa
*editions*

Europa Editions
1 Penn Plaza, Suite 6282
New York, N.Y. 10019
www.europaeditions.com
info@europaeditions.com

Library of Congress Cataloging in Publication Data is available
ISBN 978-1-60945-666-5

Naspini, Sacha
Nives

Book design by Emanuele Ragnisco
www.mekkanografici.com

Cover photo:
"Sixteen years in Caminino" 1956.
Courtesy of Maria Mangiavacchi (pictured)

Prepress by Grafica Punto Print – Rome

Printed in the USA

# NIVES

Anteo Raulli went out with the swill for the hogs, but it was him and not the slop that ended up in the trough, face-down, felled by a stroke. When he wasn't back home ten minutes later, Nives leaned out of the kitchen window and saw him there with the hog bucket beside him and Cyclamen, who didn't fully grasp the question at hand but seemed fine with that, starting to chew on his master's ear.

"Scumbag!" she yelled, flying out of the house. She grabbed her husband by the ankles and dragged him onto the gravel, out of danger. As she turned him to one side, she saw that his cheekbone was shiny, the flesh eaten away, leaving his molars exposed in a glistening grin with no blood in sight; the pig had polished him clean with lashings of his tongue. Anteo Raulli's eyes were wide open, as if he were staring at the tip of his nose. Nives stood there looking at him, the wind loosening her bun, so that her hair whipped in her face in waves. Finally, she said out loud, "I told you not to go out when there's a north wind." She turned her gaze to the pig, who responded by wagging his tail as if to say, "Can you throw me a little more?" The woman turned away. She started walking slowly towards the house. She went in, without closing the door behind her. A moment later, she came out again, her two hands clutching St. Francis—that was what the Raullis called their hunting rifle. "Come here, my beauty," she murmured to herself, clicking the safety catch with her thumb. The pig must have felt a chill in the air: he started stomping around in the muck, his back juddering. By the time Nives reached the pigsty, Cyclamen's grunts were sharp barks, some of them high-pitched squeals. He was about to make a run for the pen but was suddenly hypnotized by the rifle barrel the woman was pointing at him. The shot hit him between the eyes; Cyclamen collapsed on one side, his stiff trotters spasming. And yet, you don't need to be an expert to know that pigs should be slaughtered without their knowing it. Otherwise, stress breaks down the muscle and ruins the meat. And the skin.

Nives didn't shed a tear, not even at the funeral. Unlike her daughter, who had come home from France and turned into a siren, wailing all the way from mortuary to sermon to crematorium. She didn't cry when she got home, either. In fact, she kept pace with the appetites of her son-in-law and grandchildren, who never failed to show up with a craving for her home-made ravioli, and, as soon as she had changed out of her good clothes, there she was rummaging through the kitchen cupboards and drawers and ripping open a bag of flour.

"Mamma, we need to think about what you should do," her daughter whined, her nose wet and snotty.

Nives rolled her eyes, "Laura, if you say that one more time, I'll put my head in the oven. I have everything I need here. What do you think I should do? Come and live with you in the Languedoc? It would be like living on Mars. I can hardly pronounce your husband and kids' names. At the age of sixty-six, it's hard to uproot yourself. In any case, who would take care of the animals?"

She had to restrain herself because, if she'd followed her instincts, the conversation would have taken a different turn. Instead, she continued the conversation in her head. "You two have an eye for selling the farm; that's what it is. Renting out the fields is not enough for you, even though you suck up the income every month, right enough. The Bandini family wires the money and— whoosh—it vanishes over the Pyrenees. All that fuss at the sight of your father in a coffin with his face bandaged up, and next thing I know you're busy calculating how to holiday from one Christmas to the next. I can imagine the little Frenchman bleating with anticipation."

They stayed a week. When it was time to say goodbye, her daughter cranked up the tears again because she was upset at leaving her mother in that rambling house in the middle of nowhere. "We have a lovely bedroom waiting for you," she said, throwing herself into a hug that Nives repelled by keeping her arms rigidly by her side, her thoughts repeating, "Good luck with that." She leaned down over the children. They were identical to their father: tawny-haired and taciturn. They had never been able to look their grandmother straight in the eye. They only ever started to loosen up when it was already time to leave. "See what we've come to," Nives said to herself, planting two kisses on the kids' heads, which shone in the new spring light. She held out her hand to her son-in-law. He was a champion of politeness, for sure, but he was a pillar of salt. One of those men you had to stab with a knife before getting any emotion out of them. The very opposite of her daughter, who carried on whimpering until Nives finally turned on her and snapped, "I'm not dead yet." She'd said it partly for a laugh, and partly to let it out. But

Laura didn't take it well. It must have sounded like a sick joke so soon after her bereavement. Her face darkened, as if touched to her quick in an obscene way. "Ciao, Mamma," she sighed, dragging out the final kiss on her mother's cheek. The family clambered into the giant rental car. Nives watched them as they drove down the dirt track and disappeared onto the country road. The kids didn't turn around to wave goodbye from the back window. All that was left was a cloud of dust, which only lasted a few minutes. Then Poggio Corbello went back to what it had always been: a place closed to outsiders. Nives looked back to the trough where her husband's days had unexpectedly come to an end. She wondered how the Catani family were doing. They must have made a mint after twenty years in the slaughtering business. Following the tragedy, they'd honed in like missiles to pick up Cyclamen, but she still hadn't gotten the payment for the 280 pounds of hog meat. "Every sale is an ordeal," she muttered. And went inside.

For the first time, she wasn't able to sleep a wink. While her family had been there, she hadn't had any trouble, not even with the shock of tragedy in the air. Now, she lay there on her side of the bed and suddenly knew why: when she closed her eyes, she felt funny, as if the familiar room might change into something else while she slept. All at once, it felt unacceptable that the world could carry on going about its own business. It was as if Anteo was lying there next to her. She was terribly tired, and on two occasions nearly succumbed to her exhaustion, but if she so much as started to let the moorings slip away, her eyes would spring open again and she would come awake with a jolt and a heaving heart. This was compounded by a nauseating sensation, which luckily only lasted a few minutes, of not knowing exactly where she was. Odd, as there was really no mistaking it. She had lived on the hillock for just under half a century. There was nothing untoward in that place that could trouble the waters. The old house where she was born, so full of vivid memories, might have put her out of sorts, but that was truly a lifetime ago. It was during the second delirium of twilight sleep that she had a fright: someone was calling her. She heard her husband's voice clearly, as if from the next room, calling "Nives!" A timbre that had punctuated her life, day after day, from her girlhood to now. She thought about it this way throughout the night, putting on a brave face until she heard the first calls of the sparrows. "Anteo watched me grow up, from twenty to over sixty. A half-dream that feels like a hallucination is normal enough; I'm no monster."

When she went to look at herself in the bathroom mirror, she almost said out loud, "Who the hell is this?" The bad night stayed with her as she did the rounds to check on the animals. She fought back a tremor under her skin. Her side vision was watery.

The hutches started shaking as she approached, the rabbits competing madly to be first in line. She went over to the side of the house with her bucket of birdseed and lifted the latch of the chicken coop. The hens gathered into a clucking cloud. Nives went to look for Giacomina, who was always last out because of her right claw, which only had one lumpy nail. Anteo had been saying for ages that they should make broth out of the old thing, ever since that afternoon when she'd been maimed by the mutt that had gotten out of Potenti's gate. "A chewed-off claw like that could rot from one day to the next. Better in our soup than leaving her to waste." Nives shook her head. In the meantime, Giacomina was right there in front of her mistress. This was her way now. The hen looked her up and down, her head cocked a little to one side, her eyes dull and vacuous. The woman was desperately fond of that disaster-stricken expression, like a query openly asking the world, "What am I doing here? Do you have any idea?" That moment of intelligence vanished on the spot, of course, as soon as the shower of seeds landed by her beak, and she started pecking. In order to eat and stay upright at the same time, she was forced to keep her left wing lifted a little to balance her injured right leg. Nives spoke to her softly, "My friend, that's the story of my life for as long as I can remember." She stood watch, making sure that the unfortunate creature could eat, and that her companions didn't steal her food. Next she went to work on the vegetable garden.

She soon realized that solitude changed everything about life in the countryside. Each hour passed like a slow-motion smack in the teeth with a shovel; her usual chores took an abnormal turn. From the start, Nives accepted these changes bitterly. "Am I not enough for myself?" she asked herself. Discovering that she may not have been so late in life was a blow she could have done without. Her tasks were more burdensome with the knowledge that what was not shared was lost. Especially the little things, the nothings, like drinking a glass of water. Not even a dog to say, "What's up with this thirst?" for no reason, just to make conversation. Meaning: I see you; you exist. Not having a living soul around to see her made her feel like a ghost.

Nives ate her dinner on the sofa in front of the big TV.

After eating, she drank a drop more than usual, until she felt calmer. Every now and again, however, she glanced across the room towards the corridor and the bedroom. The idea of getting into her nightdress made her stomach shrivel to the size of a pinhead.

Three days later, she opened the front door, her face dry and her bun lopsided. Her baggy work sweater looked massive on her, like an evacuee's smock. Her rubber boots made the gravel crunch, but she felt as if her feet weren't touching the ground. If she turned her neck too fast, she felt like she was going to faint, and she'd say to herself, "I wish! At least I'd get a quarter of an hour's rest." Then she remembered how she'd found Anteo. She hated the idea that the chickens might peck out her eyes in a feeding frenzy.

In the end, she was forced to face up to the fact: it was because she'd been abandoned. During the day she could put up with it one way or another, as she was kept busy with the animals and all the rest. When night fell, a deep well opened in her. It wasn't normal fear; she knew that. Her anguish went elsewhere. As soon as she became drowsy, she would find herself gripping onto her covers, heaving like a bull. The disorientation of sleeplessness sharpened her perception of things, which made her want to eat her heart out. She thought she felt Anteo toss and turn in bed, for example. Or she would hear the sharp explosion of a loud fart echoing around the room. "It was just me," Nives told herself. "Letting my nerves go loosened my asshole, and I gave myself a fright." Her eyes would snap open if she brushed the sheet with her hand, because it felt like she was receiving a caress in the dead of night. She had pins and needles all over. Insomnia gave her that strange feeling that her skin was as thin as tracing paper. Or, worse, that it was evaporating into thin air. The death mask she saw in the mirror every morning spoke volumes. She was a ghost: no curlers in her hair, skin like wrinkled parchment, and shriveled cheeks. She didn't even look like herself when she stuck her dentures back in.

She started to stare at the telephone. She had conversations with it out loud, as if the thing were a person. "You think you're tempting me? For all I care, you can die there on that side table." Or "Nobody's ever seen Nives Cillerai blathering into a telephone, so there's no point in staring at me like that." She usually won battles of this kind by thinking about how the bill would skyrocket if she dialed a phone number on the other side of the Alps. She would get angry at herself when the phone rang in the evening and she found herself running down the corridor to answer it. "Hello?" she'd gasp, her breath stuck in her throat. On the other end, Laura would listen silently for a few seconds. "Are you doing okay, Mom?" she'd ask, skipping the preliminaries. "Couldn't be better!" Nives would answer. At times, she'd catch a glimpse of herself reflected in the picture that had been hanging there for ages, which they'd bought in Venice in '84. What she saw were bull's eyes, sticking out like torpedoes. "What time is it in the land of the cheese-eaters?" Her daughter counted to ten and said, "The room is here waiting. Waiting for you." Nives scoffed. "Tell the room to rest in peace."

There were times when she didn't even realize she'd dialed the number for Bandini, who not only rented the land from them but had also been a dear friend for an eternity. She'd see him arrive in his little pickup with the week's shopping. "Graziano, who sent you?" she'd ask as she joined him in the clearing. He'd stop and look at her, thinking she looked off-kilter, then pull down the tailgate and unload the shopping. After carrying everything inside into the larder, as a prize, he sat down to his usual glass of vermouth at ten o'clock in the morning. That was when he'd come up with something to say as bait. "So, what's it like living here without poor old Anteo's foul cussing?"

She'd shrug. "I feel like a princess."

"A mouse princess, more like," he'd say, looking around the messy kitchen with all the surfaces covered in crumbs, papers, and oily stains. "It's so quiet . . . in your place I would have pulled my ears off already."

Nives chuckled. "It's a sounding board for thoughts."

"Is that good?"

"Is it bad?"

"There are so many traps you can fall into . . . As they say, if you see everything black, the black will see you."

"Let's see who has the last laugh."

Having to be witty with her friend ate her up alive. When he closed the door behind him, it felt like a mountain falling on her head. She sometimes had to sit down in an armchair for a second until her knees stopped wobbling. She would even doze off fleetingly, as if she had fainted, and then wake up yelling, "Fucking bitch!" She would then go and look at her wedding photo, which had always occupied the middle shelf of the dresser, with the good dinner service that had been used no more than three times in as many years. "Look what you did to me," she'd snap at her young, handsome husband with his thin moustache and actor's smile. Nives would keep this up for a few more seconds before melting into waves of nostalgia. But she never shed a tear.

It was during one of these rants when, dejected to the bone, her eyes strayed to the right, where there was a picture of a woman, all blond, curly hair. Her gaze rested on her parents in their frame—she'd always seen them as guardian angels. She spoke to her mother, who couldn't have been more than twenty in the photograph. "Fiammetta, look how beautiful you are . . ." she murmured. "And look at me." At that moment, she remembered a story that had always made her laugh when she was a child.

It was during the war, when handsome Roberto had been sent to the front to fight, leaving his wife, mother, and sisters to die of heartbreak. Nives saw again how emotional her mother got whenever she described that winter: alone, in their humble home still redolent of orange blossom. No more than a girl, but she was determined to wait within those walls for her man to come back. She slept in the cold, the candlewick burning down in no time at all. "A love fairy," Nonna Landa called her. Letters arrived so rarely she wanted to tear her hair out. The nights were dark, interrupted by the loud explosions that echoed throughout the small town from the air-raids over the cities. Fiammetta was terrified. She hid under her blanket and counted the minutes. One day, she came up with an idea: she caught a cricket and put it in a box on her bedside table. It kept her company. She spoke to it. By reassuring it, she reassured herself. For half a century she'd told the story of how the little critter had saved a young woman from the torment of waiting, which had consumed her so badly that her hair had permanently turned gray.

First, Nives went to the rabbit hutches. She picked up a cage that was going rotten and gave it a good rinse. Then she opened the door of the chicken coop. The hens were lined up on the straw like abbesses. To begin with, they reacted badly to all that light at such an ungodly hour; some behaved as though they had been told to lay an egg but were too constipated to do so, having been surprised like that in the early hours of their sleep. The cockerel strutted up and down as if the coop had been invaded by Martians. Nives didn't hesitate: she ducked her head and dived to the back of the pen where she found the bird that she'd been looking for among those who had carried on sleeping despite the commotion. She grabbed her by the base of her neck and whisked her away.

Giacomina didn't come to until she was already in the cage. She lifted her head instinctively and pecked at the iron mesh.

"What brio!" Nives said from under the covers, tapping the seed feeder twice: *flick flick*. And suddenly the hen didn't care two hoots that she was no longer surrounded by the walls of the coop where she'd been born. She tucked into the tube without hesitation.

The first thing Nives thought when she woke up was, "I slept like a grouse in goose down." It made her laugh. With Giacomina by her side, her sleep was as undisturbed as a saint's.

The hen was there in her place, standing to attention, her silhouette outlined against the lamp. As usual, she had the air of a half-crazed evacuee; at the same time, she was a bit of a battle-ax. Nives could see the tip of an egg of miserly proportions popping out from her derriere. It was a little too blueish, almost like a pigeon's. "It's the change," her mistress said, stretching in her bed for ten more minutes.

From one day to the next, she started jeering at the telephone relentlessly, "You can look at me as long as you
want, but you'll still be stuck there barking at the moon."
Her words came out with enough force to give giants the
shivers. She took care of the vegetable garden and the animals in short order, then did the same inside the house,
even taking on the windows. Such a deep clean hadn't
been seen since '71, when a twenty-year-old Nives had still
been trying to impress a husband who disappeared into
the fields at first light.

In short, she was reborn. Bustling about here and there,
she took Giacomina with her, as safely preserved in her little cage as a delicate flower in an urn is protected from the
elements. "If I'd thrown myself at the mercy of the stupid
doctor, he'd have stuffed me with pills and strong drops,"
she said, looking at her friend, who was always rather
removed from her surroundings. "Instead, you were everything I needed."

That evening, Laura found her mother reborn; her
spirit that of a young girl. Once, to shake off her doubts,
she had to ask her, "Mom, have you been drinking?" Nives
burst into a hearty laugh. She looked at Giacomina scam-
pering around the living room, where she would let her
out to stretch her legs a little. "Worse," she replied play-
fully. She enjoyed alarming her daughter.

Nives even took the hen into the bathroom. Whenever
her mistress settled down to watch TV, Giacomina
perched on the armchair, which still held the shape of
Anteo. It was fun to watch her there, her half-crazed eye
cocked at the quiz shows or the bluster of politicians ripping one another to shreds to the sound of "the statistics
say that . . ." Nives commented on the outrages of these

over-paid wordmongers out loud. "What a world we live in, my friend." There was sometimes a cluck in return. The woman nodded back, "I agree."

Grooming the bird was no more disgusting than when she'd had to struggle with her late husband's thick toe nails, especially in recent times. He would present her with claws that could easily have bored holes into his shoes, the dirt encrusted in the folds of his toes since Easter. Nives liked polishing her friend's feathers; she used a damp cloth that she also rubbed her beak with. She soon grew used to the particular smell that began to mark the house.

When she was in the vegetable patch, she'd find snails in the earth and set them aside in a bowl. Once she was done gardening, she rinsed them out well in the outdoor sink and gave Giacomina a plate of freshly -made spaghetti for dinner. The hen repaid her by laying beautiful eggs that Nives drank fresh or scrambled—the way she liked them best. A perfect give and take.

There were few critical moments. Foremost was when she surprised herself with this realization: she had replaced Anteo with a crippled old hen. What made that weird was the following: with Giacomina by her side, there was nothing about her husband that she missed. She was assailed by a sense of despondency that she didn't know what to do with, telling herself, "I gave my life to a man I've been able to replace with a chicken." It made her feel dirty. But also wasted. She tested herself by looking back to things that at one time would make her feel weak with longing, but they didn't stir her blood as they used to. Anteo bringing her the first bunch of poppies. Anteo holding her in the crook of his arm at the fall fair. Anteo looking at the explosion of sunflowers and saying, "They make less light than you." Nothing. The kind of serviceable smile you would give little dogs begging for food from your plate, that was all. She didn't give an inch even when she leafed through the family album. She recited out loud, "This is when we won the dance contest in '79 . . . This is our thirtieth anniversary dinner . . ." Giacomina, perfectly composed, squatted next to her on the velvet cushion— the nice overstuffed one her husband had always claimed for himself. The hen poked her beak at one picture in particular. "That's Domenico, in name and in fact. A cousin, on Mom's side. They used to call him Dromedary, just to give you an idea how keen he was to waste so much as an hour at work. Then he moved to Venezuela to become a taxi driver, and I never saw him again."

The first time Bandini returned with the week's supplies, he found the hen underfoot while he sipped his vermouth. "Nives, one of your animals has gotten into the house," he said, about to shoo the bird away with a good kick. Nives swooped over to his side, "Stop!" She plucked Giacomina up and held her to her breast. Graziano watched the scene, his heart shrinking to the size of a grape. Not knowing what to say, he emptied his glass in one gulp and left.

The news soon spread to France. That evening Laura asked her straight out, "Mom, is it true there's a hen living with you in the house?" Nives mentally threw a poison dart at that busybody, Bandini, but she knew at heart that he'd only told her daughter out of sincere affection and concern. "Well, what about you, sleeping with a snail-eater who never says a word?" Her daughter didn't react to the provocation. "It's not normal." Nives felt the jab deep down. "Little Miss, let this be clear: I can keep whatever company I like. Focus on funneling in all the rents from the fields; something you are remarkably good at. Meanwhile, I can invite an ass into my living room if I feel like it," she said, and hung up.

Roosting on the armchair, Giacomina watched the Tide commercial. On screen, the spin cycle was visible through the washing machine's porthole. She gaped at it, transfixed. That was how Nives came upon her. The hen's eyes had gone blank.

At times like these, she'd usually let things take their own course. She was scared she'd traumatize the bird if she shook her, like with sleepwalkers. After five minutes, she cleared her throat a few times to no effect. The TV program had changed. Nives got up and gently touched Giacomina's wing. "Has someone thrown a spell on you?" she murmured. Not even a twitch. In the end, she went for the clincher: she grabbed the zapper and switched the TV off.

Giacomina looked wooden. "Come on, pet," her mistress pleaded, clucking like a mother. If this went on any longer, the hen's eyes would turn to glass. She didn't think she'd blinked since the phone call. The bird was perched there, wearing her usual demented expression, her beak hanging slightly open, as if she had taken a turn. Nives bent over her, prodding her more insistently, "What, are you the waking dead?"

Most people would burst out laughing seeing an animal pretending to be a statue. But Nives felt her heart race. She picked the hen up carefully. It was like handling a crystal ornament. She tried shaking her. A funny sound came out of Giacomina's throat, like the thrumming of a string drum: *ga*. But the hen was still a statue. Nives shook her again, as if she were rocking a newborn baby: *ga, ga, ga.* She stuck her back in the armchair and went into the kitchen to fetch an iron pot and a ladle. "I'll soon wake you up," she muttered, banging the pot—not too hard to begin with. No reaction. She came one step closer. Another bang, with more force. Giacomina squatted there, frozen. Her mistress even thought of going to bother St. Francis and shooting off a round, right there, a yard away. But she stuck with the pot, banging so hard that it rang inside her, right down to her marrow. Not a feather was ruffled.

Where would she ever find another egg-laying friend with a disposition like hers? Nives had already realized that Giacomina's charm was unique; she needed her as a bridge between Anteo's death and the shape of her now, redrawn in her solitude, and it wasn't something she could teach any old bird at the drop of a hat. She was scared she'd be plunged back into those twilight sleeps that used to drain her. Or worse, that France would win, which, in short, meant spending the rest of her days on Mars, where she wouldn't even be able to order a coffee for herself.

She strode over to the telephone table and picked up the copybook they'd always jotted their phone numbers in. She found what she was looking for under the B's: Bottai. He was the vet who'd always come to check up on the animals. Nives looked at the time: it was just past eight. Loriano was a good doctor, but he had a drinking problem; everybody knew. He started first thing in the morning and carried on poisoning his liver until dinner time—after a day with his hands up goats' and heifers' asses and inside their gums, he put himself out of his misery with a last glass before collapsing into bed as soon as the theme tune from the evening news was over. The news on Channel 4; the one the oldies prefer.

His wife answered the phone, "Hello?"

"Donatella, sorry to ambush you like this. It's Nives here."

The woman on the other end of the line took a moment to connect the voice to the name. "My dear, what a surprise!" She was suddenly reminded of everything that had happened, Anteo's death and all the rest. She gathered her thoughts and acted more pleased than usual to be in touch with her friend. "Imagine, I was thinking of you today! I was just saying to myself, 'Maybe one of these afternoons . . . ?'"

Nives wasn't in the mood for any sweet-talking. She was a little sorry to interrupt the serenade just as it was gearing up, but this was an emergency. "Is Loriano home?"

Donatella cleared her throat. "He's in there," she muttered, already changing her tone. "I was in the bedroom a few minutes ago. He's as stiff as a mummy."

"Can you call him for me?"

There was an indecipherable mumbling, provoked by her embarrassment at having to own up to the evidence: her husband was sloshed. Donatella gave it a shot, hoping to avoid having to make excuses. "You could try tomorrow morning, maybe? You know he goes to bed with the chickens."

"That's what I'm calling about."

"Have they caught an infection?"

"There's an emergency."

Rebuffing a new widow was a sin that might make the rounds of the entire neighborhood on the tongues of tittle-tattlers. Donatella wondered whether to pass the call to the bedroom phone but immediately thought better of it. Loriano should get up and regain a modicum of consciousness. Her teeth clenched, she said, "One moment."

Nives could hear noises from the other side of the receiver: the clacking of heels on floor tiles, creaking, curses. An important saint's name being taken in vain. Nives looked over at Giacomina on the armchair. She looked artificial.

There was a commotion as things crashed to the floor, followed by Donatella's voice yelling as if to the moon, "Imbecile!" Until, finally, a hand must have reached out and roughly grabbed the receiver. Bottai's voice was mangy with sleep and phlegm, "Hello Nives . . . my condolences."

He had already given them profusely on the day of the funeral. She felt as desperate as someone watching her train pulling out of the station.

"Loriano, listen."

"Tell me."

"I have a hen."

"A hen."

"She's taken a funny turn."

"Who?"

"The hen, I mean."

"The hen has taken a funny turn?"

"Yes. How do I wake her up?"

"How do you wake her up?"

"I'm asking you."

On the other end of the line there was a moment's pause. Nives imagined the empty gaze of that vet who thought of nothing but demijohns of wine. Finally, Bottai came back to himself.

"Is this a riddle?"

"Loriano, can you listen to me?"

"I'm listening."

"I have a hen who's gotten stuck in a Tide commercial."

"Tide."

"Exactly."

"The one with the pods?"

"Yes, that one."

"Can you pour me an inch?"

"What?"

"I was talking to Donatella."

"I drummed on the pot, but it was no use."

"You drummed on the pot."

"It was no use."

"Listen, I'm not feeling too well right now and—"

"Loriano, it's important. Can you tell me what to do? I'll pay you for the disturbance if you come over."

Hearing there may be some cash in the offing, Bottai tried to regain the high ground. A few coins are better than nothing, after all. But he was really at a loss.

"Nives, I don't understand what you're saying. You were talking about dishwasher detergent."

"Laundry detergent! Tide."

"Tide."

"That commercial that's running right now, with the spin cycle at full speed."

"I think I've seen it."

"Giacomina's seen it, too."

"Eh?"

"I don't know. She just sits there, as still as a photograph. She doesn't even blink."

Bottai took a deep breath, as if he'd been running, and

tried to process the alcohol he'd drunk over the day in order to grasp onto some semblance of himself.

"Nives, do I know this Giacomina?"

"She's the hen I was talking about at the beginning."

"Ah, a hen."

"She watched the Tide commercial and turned to stone."

"Look, you know if I wake up after falling asleep, I get palpitations! Bring me an inch and I'll be fine."

"What?"

"I was talking to Donatella."

"I was telling you about my little pet."

"The hen."

"Yes."

"She took a funny turn watching the Tide."

"Exactly."

"And what am I supposed to do about it?"

"You're the doctor, aren't you? If it goes on any longer, she'll rot in my living room."

"You keep the hen in your living room?"

"I can keep her wherever I like. The point is, we need to wake her up."

"What if she brings lice into the house?"

"She brings calm into the house."

"These animals rake around all day in their own shit."

"I know lots of people who do worse."

"You're telling me . . . Listen, we've done all the vaccinations, right?"

"Yes."

"What about sleep, how is she doing on that count?"

"She's a regular chicken. At midday she feasts on beetles from the vegetable garden. I take care of her better than if she were the Pope."

Bottai was sucking on his drink, you could hear it over the phone. Light was beginning to filter through to his brain, penetrating his befuddlement. He had been right: one glass of wine had done the trick, though he was still slurring his words.

"What about her feathers?"

"You should see her. She looks like porcelain."

"She must be hypnotized."

"Who?"

"Giancarlina, or whatever her name is."

"Giacomina."

"Yes, her."

"Giacomina is hypnotized?"

"They're stupid creatures. It can happen."

Nives couldn't contain herself: "Speak for yourself."

Loriano cleared his throat. "No, no, I just mean—"

"Is it dangerous?"

"I've never heard of a hen dying of it. If anything, somebody might think she's dead and stick her in the oven with potatoes. She wouldn't even notice."

"Holy smokes!" Nives imagined Giacomina on the spit and, for a second, her knees gave way. And yet, she had picked many a chicken bone clean in her day. Not that she wanted to boast, but her chicken stew was pretty good. "That makes me feel sick."

"It'll pass. It's a condition."

"And if she doesn't wake up?"

Bottai gave a deep sigh. He was growing tired of the woman's nonsense. "Try shaking her."

"I have. I drummed the pot, too."

"Ah, yes. The pot—"

"I also picked her up. It was no good. She's bewitched."

"She'll get over it."

"And if she doesn't?"

"Nives, what do you want me to say?"

"What about smelling salts?"

"Good idea! Try them."

"Anyway, will you come and see her tomorrow?"

"Yes, I'm coming now."

"Now?"

"I was talking to Donatella. She's gone to bed, and that's bad news for me."

"Donatella can't go to bed?"

"She snores. Once she starts, it's over for me: I can never get to sleep again."

"Is that my fault?"

"It's Alfredina's fault, or whatever her name is."

"Giacomina."

"Yes, her."

"For me, she's manna from heaven. Thanks to her, I haven't had to pack my bags and move to the Languedoc. Or to the loony bin, or somewhere even worse. As for sleep: I couldn't get any sleep at all before. After a week without sleep, I felt like I was walking in the clouds. With her on my bedside table, I sleep right through the night. It's sad, isn't it? As sad as everything else."

"No, what are—"

"You can talk: you've got that brass band to keep you company."

"I usually knock myself out with drink first."

"A bad habit."

"And what isn't?"

There was a moment's pause as they sat and listened to one another breathing. Their last exchange had created a strange embarrassment. When the silence became too awkward, Nives said, "Loriano?"

"Yes."

"I'm asking you as a doctor: is it normal to replace a husband with a chicken, and not to miss anything about the husband, not even for half a minute?"

Bottai rolled his eyes. "Grief plays tricks on you. You'll see." A light bulb suddenly clicked in his head. "What did you mean when you said she's crippled?"

"Just that: one leg is crooked."

"That must be it, then. Is there any pus? Is it infected?"

"Not at all. It's an old story, at least a year old. She was left with a gammy leg. Like Favilli, who lost the three fingers of his right hand, the ones he left in the lathe. He's not dead, right? He drives the tractor alright, though maybe he shouldn't!"

"Is she still asleep?"

Nives turned around to look into the living room. "It's like she's sculpted."

"Lucky her!"

"She's starting to spook me."

"Try smelling salts."

"But you'll come tomorrow, won't you?"

Loriano paused. Then he gave in to the temptation. "Listen, are you saying it works?"

"What?"

"This thing with a hen on your bedside table?"

"What do you mean?"

"Are you saying it makes you sleep better?"

"I was reborn. My poor old ma used a cricket."

"A cricket?"

"It saved her nerves."

"A cricket."

"She kept it in a jar. It was called Guglielmo. Whenever she told me about it, I laughed and laughed."

"I bet."

"But it did save her nerves. She talked to it."

"What did she say?"

"I don't know. I hadn't arrived yet. In any case, I tell Giacomina stories."

Bottai's head was spinning, both from the wine and from the bombshells being dropped from the Raulli household on the other end of the phone. With every word she said, the woman pulled a wild-card out of thin air. Once the widow's words were aired, anything could happen. "For example?"

"The tale of Giuccomatto. Keeping Giacomina on my bedside table has made me remember a whole flurry of stories. They were Nonna Landa's stories, handed down from a century ago." Nives could hear a rhythmic noise across the line. She listened harder. "Has a cicada gotten into your house? It's not even the season."

"It's Donatella. Now you know what I mean."

"Poor thing."

"Poor thing? What about me?"

"It sounds like a moped."

"It sounds like the life sentence it is."

"You're exaggerating. She's a good woman."

"No arguments here. But she even bores into the eardrums of our upstairs neighbor."

Nives gathered her thoughts. "Pagliuchi."

"Yes, him. But I'm just saying."

"How handsome he was when he was young. When he walked by, all the girls went gaga."

Loriano had no idea what to say. In the end, all he could manage was an incomprehensible, "Eh . . ." This felt like a good moment to try and get away, "Nives, I—"

"When he was a boy, he used to go into town and play the gigolo."

"Yes, so I hear."

"People do what they can to get by."

"Those were the days. Nives, now I—"

"That business with Rosaltea was a nasty shock."

"Mother Mary, look what you made me remember—"

"Everyone said she wasn't all there. The truth is, she was just crazy with love."

"They're things you can't really explain, they are."

"After being dumped so many times, one day she threw herself from the belfry."

"I was there."

"What?"

"The day it happened; I was there in the piazza."

"Did you see her fall?"

"Almost. I was having a cup of coffee at the bar. I can see it so clearly: it was market day. I was talking to Tancredi, God bless his soul. Suddenly, there was a dull thud, as if someone had thrown a bag of cement down from a third-floor window."

"It wasn't a bag of cement."

"No."

"It was Rosa."

"In a nightie," Bottai added.

"I didn't know that."

"I dreamed about it for ages."

"When they told me, I fainted."

"You and everyone else in the neighborhood."

There was a heartbeat's silence. Bottai was about to worm his way into the pause to bring the phone call to an end—what with hens and crickets the conversation had taken a turn that would have robbed even an angel of their sleep.

Nives beat him to it. "I wonder what it's like."

Loriano longed for a rifle shot to end things. "What?"

"Living with death on your conscience."

"Don't talk nonsense. What led Rosaltea to the belfry was her illness. Renato had nothing to do with it."

"Unless the man is a monster, he must have asked himself a few questions. If he'd welcomed her overtures, maybe Rosa would still be alive today."

"You can't command love."

"I heard dear old Pagliuchi didn't mind diving under her skirts every now and again."

"Nives, we were boys, not pieces of wood."

"You know, some poor woman is drooling all over you and what do you do? You exploit her, out of greed. For you, it's a cheap thrill. For her, it feels like a chance. One minute later, you're riding another mare. Dear old Renato Pagliuchi has the girl on his conscience alright. In the meantime, as far as I've heard, he never even got married. Am I wrong?"

Loriano had to make an effort not to hang up. "You're not wrong," he exhaled, exhausted.

"All those fireworks when he was young, and now he's all alone, like a dog, already looking old age in the face."

Bottai didn't want to give in to the woman, not on this point. "He looks fine to me."

"How do you know? Maybe inside he's hollowed out?"

"It doesn't look like it. He gets up early, goes off on

long walks as if he were still young. He's only beginning to
go bald at the back of his head, whereas for me it started
ages ago. Driving coaches doesn't seem to have worn him
out one bit. I'll tell you something more: women still look
at him, even women twenty years his junior."

Nives took in his defiant reaction with venom stuck in
her throat.

"Which only means he's still thinking with what's below
his belt. You need to know that life's not one big hand-job.
You're all pathetic."

Bottai realized he was enjoying himself. Making this old
friend, who had woken him up so rudely, choke on
Pagliuchi was a great way to get his own back. "We're *all*
pathetic? What have I done?"

"You men are all of a kind."

He wouldn't let go. He'd found her soft spot and continued to prod her there. "You seem quite upset. What do
you care about Renato?" He couldn't stop himself from
going further. "It must mean you got burned as well." He
regretted saying this immediately. It wasn't a nice thing to
say to a woman who'd just been widowed.

Nives came out with the last words Bottai ever imagined he would hear. She uttered them calmly. "For that
matter, not just me, there's Donatella, too."

Some of the alcohol that had been pickling him evapo-
rated on the spot. "Excuse me?"

"We were girls, not pieces of wood."

"Excuse me?"

"That's what I said."

"My Donatella? With Pagliuchi?" Loriano choked
back his laughter. He made it last a little too long, trying to
make it sound spontaneous. "Nives, what are you saying?"

"Ask that horn-player in your bedroom. Ask her how certain summer afternoons at the old gully tasted."

"You're joking, right?"

"July '66, to be precise. I could be wrong, though. It might have been August."

Bottai threw himself into calculating. He counted with his fingers. It was easy to work out, but he was so groggy it took him three goes to confirm it. In the end, it was clear. As if he were thinking out loud, he said, "She was fifteen."

"Exactly like yours truly."

Loriano knew he hadn't been the first to touch his wife. There had been Nando, for example. There'd been another guy, whose name he couldn't remember, too. They'd been short-lived affairs that lasted a few months, at most a year. As for him, he'd attracted her attention when she was twenty. He'd had no idea that Renato Pagliuchi had also stuck his nose into certain sweet places. There was nothing sacred about it, but it still upset him. "She never told me," he said. "I reckon you're mistaken."

"Sorry, but would there be anything wrong with it?"

Bottai took pride in sounding relaxed. "Nothing, for goodness sake."

"You seem quite upset. It must mean you got burned."

Loriano decided to tone things down. He saw the trap he'd fallen into. He felt sorry for Nives: there, in that house on Poggio Corbello, with only a spellbound hen for company. She wouldn't get off the phone. She'd thrown herself into upending a marriage that was sailing serenely toward a half century the first chance she got. While hers no longer existed. It was no skin off his nose to go along with the poor woman. His hangover was sinking down into his nether regions; all that was left was a sense of shock that made his face fizz. Anyway, who cared? There was nothing blasphemous about Donatella having had a bit of fun in the fields. He looked towards the bedroom, from whence came the snores of an ogress. "More power to you," he thought, adding out loud, "You had a good time. I'm happy for you."

"The trick was not to get all mushy."

"What?"

"With Pagliuchi, I mean."

"Ah, him again."

"You got on top of him and had your twenty minutes of fun, as God intended. If you started writing love letters, he would drop you on the spot."

"At least he made himself clear."

"You'd have to be an idiot to get stuck with a tool like him. Renato Pagliuchi was sculpted by golden hands, but who would ever have taken him seriously? Just thinking about setting up a family with him was enough to sprout a pair of horns. It was more fun for us girlfriends—us bad girls, I mean—to go somewhere and talk about him. You know, like girls of that age do."

"Bitches in heat," Loriano thought. All of a sudden, he felt a thud in his stomach because he imagined Donatella there in the group.

Nives concluded, "Wanting something exclusive with Pagliuchi was like signing your death warrant."

Bottai spoke without thinking, "That's what happened with Rosa."

There was silence. Like before a storm, when the monsters are unleashed from the depths. Nives grabbed on to one of the monster's horns. "What are you saying?"

"No, nothing."

"It was different with her. You know she was sick."

"True."

"She was obsessed. She wanted him all to herself."

"May she rest in peace."

"With a dead husband, do you really want to hand me this cross to bear, too?"

"Which?"

"You know."

"Nives, really, don't—"

"It wasn't our fault."

"I didn't say it was. I don't think it was."

"Renato carried on with her. He pitied her, and, anyway, she was beautiful."

"There's nothing else to say."

"We girls would go to the gully with him, but we didn't want to hurt her."

"Okay, calm down now."

"You see, now I'm scared."

"Of what?"

"Of seeing Rosaltea here in her nightie with her head split open."

"There's no one there."

"I've summoned her now. I might go into the bathroom and see her in the mirror."

"Nives, don't talk nonsense."

"Maybe she's the one who put a curse on my hen. As soon as I hang up, she'll open her beak and start talking to me."

"It's just hypnotized."

"It's been going on for a while. This is what she wanted: for me to call you, dig up things from fifty years ago, and then make me die of a heart attack. Have you thought of that?"

"What?"

"No, you haven't thought of it."

"What?"

"Fernanda Demaria, for example."

Loriano remembered his dear friend's funeral, a year ago already. "Now, what does that poor woman—"

"Lorenza Tucci. That's without counting the ones who were ten years older or more, like Bonelli. Do you remember Bonelli? Or that big woman, Vanda? They're all dead."

"Nives . . ."

"Rosa's already started."

Loriano couldn't control it. A shiver ran through him, like a comb going the wrong way. This was followed by a combination of amusement and pity. The woman's forced solitude had conjured up unexpected ghosts. "Are you serious?"

"She cuts us down with her scythe one by one. In my case, it started with Anteo. You should have seen his test results from the clinic: they came back perfect; they were so clear that you could see through them."

Bottai attempted to do his job properly. It appeared he was being called upon to perform a task that was much more delicate than diagnosing the condition of a hen trapped inside a commercial. "Death is perfectly natural," he said. "Take Bonelli, for example. Does her passing at almost eighty seem like the curse of some spirit? If there's anything that punishes the living, it is life itself. We don't need to bring ghosts into it. In any case, it has another name."

"Like?"

"I don't know. A 'guilty conscience,' for example."

"Guilty conscience."

"For example."

"And what kind of little ghost would that be?"

"What you see. What you want to see."

Loriano had the impression that Nives had stopped to think about this for a while. The pause would have been the perfect moment to say goodnight, but he was human, after all. His friend was scared. She was regurgitating things from her past, and they were visiting her in the night, taking on the semblance of a real presence. He didn't want to have her on his conscience.

"She's already started," Nives insisted, unaffected by his words. "If she starts doing to you what she's already done to me . . . what about your prostate? How's that doing? To name just one thing."

Bottai instinctively touched his balls to ward off evil. But he had to remain rooted in fact, like a real doctor. "Let's keep our feet on the ground, shall we?"

"Aren't your capillaries popping?"

"What?"

"Around your eyes. Your cheeks, too. They're full of spidery, red blotches. It could be your blood pressure."

Loriano took a step to one side to look at himself in the mirror that hung there. It was a giant catafalque of a thing, with rusty edges. The impressive thing about it was its gilded frame. Past reflections of generations of Bottais inhabited it. The old patriarch had always said, right to the end, that the mirror went back to the beginning of the 1800s, before all the ingredients of Italy had been thrown into the stew. He saw in the reflection that he was disheveled. His jowls were firm and solid. Sometimes the friends he played Tresette with would say, "Lollo, have they put you under the press?" He laughed. But inside he was sorry he was not as fit as he used to be. He'd never been handsome, but when he was in good shape, he'd cut a dashing figure, even after he'd gone almost completely bald. On the sides, and at the back, he still had some curls. His prize feature, however, was his eyes, which were a rare silver-gray color. He dabbed at his cheekbone. The tip of his finger sunk in halfway up his nail. "I feel fine."

"It's the drink. And that pot belly. It weighs on your heart. Five steps and your ticker leaps into your throat, right? Tell me the truth."

Bottai felt the palpitations coming on. "Never felt better." It came out oddly, though, like a death rattle.

"You don't believe it yourself."

"Now you've become a doctor, have you?"

"Anyway, Donatella used to lie down in the shade of the chestnut grove."

"Good for her."

"She made poor Rosaltea sick, like many of us. Take Tucci, or Demaria . . ."

With all that business of hypnotized animals on bedside tables, escapades under the skirts of a young wife, and ghosts at ten in the evening, Loriano had gotten a little dizzy. He made a shuffling noise with his slippers on the tiles. "Nives, it really is late."

"That's how it started with Anteo; he was always tired. In his final days, you needed to fire a canon to get him out of bed in the morning."

"I have to get up at six o' clock, excuse me if—"

"*Caffe latte* and Fernet?"

"It's none of your business."

"And you don't stop slugging it down until the evening."

"That's my own business."

"That's how she's dealing with you."

"Who?"

"Rosa."

"Rosa?"

"She keeps a wide berth, but there are hundreds of bottles tied around her neck. You can't see her, and maybe you can't even hear her, though you should. But don't worry, they'll all come together."

For a moment, Loriano's breath caught in his throat. He quickly tried to imagine all he'd drunk over the course of a lifetime—he already had one foot in the grave. But he instinctively rebelled against the idea. "Nonsense. There's no ghost trying to get me to drink." Then he felt a little foolish for saying such a thing.

"You have a great job, an exceptional wife, your son Amedeo has a promising career at the bank, and you even had the grandchild of everyone's dreams a few years ago. You own your house; you have vacations at the seaside . . . what else do you want?"

Loriano hated being X-rayed like that. What did the insomniac widow want exactly? This was his reward for being a shoulder to cry on, as she vented all the trials of her solitude. He had his back against the wall. "I don't want anything."

"So, what is it?"

"How am I supposed to know—"

"Rosa."

"If you want to call it that."

"How else?"

"She keeps me company."

"She's killing you."

"As far as I know, I'm still here."

"For now."

This time the swipe was so strong that Loriano was nearly knocked sideways by it. "Can you stop this?"

"She's keeping a wide berth."

"You're talking about a ghost that kills people out of revenge. After an entire lifetime? It's a strange form of fury."

"The worst. She knows exactly the chains that bind us."

"She could take it out on Pagliuchi and that would be that. Anyway, I know what you're trying to say."

"What am I trying to say?"

"That Rosa is that thing we all have, which sometimes keeps us awake at night."

"And makes you drink."

Loriano smiled bitterly. "Okay, I have my Rosa, too. Happy now?"

"What do you think of Renato's situation, then, with no family despite his good looks?"

"Rosa."

"Precisely."

Ultimately, it was a funny way to talk about things. A bit macabre, perhaps. Bottai wasn't sure whether his friend saw the ghost as a metaphor or whether she really believed in it. He felt as though he'd reached a pause in the conversation when it would be acceptable to hang up. He thought about how his night would go. In the light of what they'd just said, uncorking a bottle and feeding his hangover was out of the question. It would be like casting the evil eye on himself. Maybe he'd pick up a book; he hadn't done that for a long time. He had to plug his ears first.

Nives incinerated every goodbye. "But with Donatella she's been more devious."

"What?"

"Look at the position she's put her in."

"Who? What?"

"Rosa, who else?"

Bottai reneged all the doubts he'd harbored until one second before. "What do you think she's done now?"

"You're right in there, shoes and all. How can you not see?"

"Nives, either say something or—"

"Just look up at the ceiling."

Goosebumps prickled Loriano's skin. He imagined looking up and seeing the poor girl from his past lying up there. In the same unnatural position that he'd seen her on that terrible day in the piazza. After a long pause, he said, "I can't see anything."

"If you were able to see through walls, you wouldn't be here."

Only then did Bottai get it. "Do you mean Pagliuchi?"

"There's Donatella's little gift."

"Nives, you've been speaking in riddles from the start—"

"The chains had to go on clanging nice and loud."

"I'm not following you."

"Of course not. You drink like a fish."

"I'm really not following you."

"Answer this question."

"Let's hear it."

"Who lived upstairs in the old days?"

Loriano had been born and raised in that building. He remembered old Ansano and his crazy wife, who was obsessed with black cats. Their house was full of them. There were two rumors going around. One was that they ate them. They coupled mothers with sons, and fathers with daughters, in a giant incestuous orgy, and then picked one out of the colony every now and again, without anyone noticing, and stuck it in the cooking pot. A custom left over from wartime, malicious tongue-waggers would say, when everyone had a taste of desperate hunger, the kind that makes you lick the walls. The other was that Norma was a witch. When Bottai was a kid, he preferred the latter theory, as did everyone else in his gang. Dazzled by these memories, he said, "We used to climb up here with our catapults. We were good at aiming stones. There were usually three of us: me, Paride De Lorenzi, and Ornello Pacchetti, a.k.a. Resisti. We would take up our positions on the side of the house and aim at the church bell."

"Fun."

"It was because in those days people didn't have watches. Norma used the bell chimes to know when to get lunch ready; at midday she'd throw the pasta in the boiling water. We waited there on the corner with our catapults loaded. Eleven o'clock came around: *ding, ding, ding* . . . on the final ring, the first of us walloped the stone over. If it missed, the next boy was ready with his elastic pulled right back. *Dong.* We'd made it midday. Norma started readying the meal. Her husband was expected back any minute."

"You drove a poor old lady crazy?"

"Ansano would come back from his workshop to find his pasta glued to the plate. He would curse her, and we would be pissing ourselves. Like Norma, though, other women got caught up in our game. When my mother fell into the trap, I stopped. My buttered *tagliolini* tasted like chalk. In those days, nothing went to waste." Loriano gave a deep sigh. "If they were here now, I'd give the old couple a big hug. All this to say, yes, I know perfectly well who lived upstairs."

Nives sharpened her tongue, unmoved. She had every intention of forging on. "As I remember it, the house was uninhabited for a long time."

"True."

"Then."

"Then Renato bought it. He sold the family house that was too big for a bachelor."

"And there he was suddenly, over your heads."

"That's right."

"Him of all people."

"Him of all people."

"With Donatella downstairs."

"Where else would she have been?"

"The same Donatella who—like many other girls at the time—used to go down to the gully. And she didn't go to pick daisies. If anything, she was interested in another kind of stalk—"

"I don't want to know what kind."

"Nice and turgid, for a start."

"Nives, please."

"They were hard years."

"In what way?"

"Of agony."

"What agony?"

"Come on, you know."

"I don't."

"You are doing your rounds, sticking your hands up

cows' cooches. And she is there, alone in the house . . . The boredom of it! There's the TV to cheer her up after her chores. Or there are the movements of a man of a certain age who's made a pact with the devil: old age hasn't even touched him. Years have gone by, but he looks the same as he did in '66.

"Donatella spies on Renato?"

"You know how it works, don't you?"

"No."

"Yes, you do."

"You tell me."

"From one day to another, you realize you've aged. There's the house, the family. In the early days, you had fire in your veins; you were ready to part the waters of the sea every step you took. When forty comes along, things are already different. At fifty, it's worse. The days grind by, and they are all the same: it's New Year's Eve and, one breath later, it's Christmas again. The only satisfaction in life is having paid all the bills."

"Thank goodness it's still like that."

"It may happen that your brain starts ticking over. Everyone knows: when life's waters are calm, anxieties sail. You start looking for a way to make up for that sense of waste. Thinking back to a fling is a way to wile the afternoon away. It's a way to dive back into the past, when life wasn't so deadly boring, and everything still lay ahead."

"Donatella thinks about Renato?" Loriano laughed out loud; this time it was sincere. "She doesn't need to; she sees him every day."

"Exactly."

"What?"

"She sees him every day."

"He lives upstairs. For twenty years, he's been the first person I say good morning to when I leave the house."

"Exactly."

"Nives, you're making me come out in a sweat. Can't you just say it?"

"Donatella was a doll when she was a girl."

"True."

"Now, she's changed."

"We all have."

"She's put on a lot of weight."

"After Amedeo, she lost her figure. It's her constitution."

"It must be frustrating."

"What can I say? She doesn't like to talk about it. I notice, though. She won't look at any mirrors. Maybe she can't stand seeing herself with all that extra flesh; she prefers an image of herself from when she was twenty. The same thing happens to me, too. Sometimes, I catch a reflection of myself in a store window and I'm shocked. "Who's that?" I ask myself. It's like a brick on your stomach. It's the same for everyone."

"Not for Renato Pagliuchi."

"He was born under a lucky star. Bully for him."

"Just think of the agony."

"Not again?"

"You know what I mean."

"No, I don't."

In fact, a second later, Loriano got it. But he didn't say so. He waited for Nives to say it. From the other end of the line, he heard the sharp retort: "It's the comparison."

"Ah, that."

"Condemned to living in the sights of that Adonis, who

used to get your juices flowing when you were a girl. He's the same as he was. You've turned into a battleship."

"Come on, don't exaggerate now."

"It must be torture."

Bottai sighed. He glanced back at the bedroom; the light was still on and the nasal concert was in full flow. He felt a wave of tenderness for the woman sleeping there. On her side of the bed, the springs were flattened out. Donatella wore a nightdress to bed; even in the summer she never went without. Loriano hadn't seen her naked for years. "She's still a beautiful woman," he said.

"No doubt about that."

Bottai murmured with a smile on his lips, "Is Renato her Rosa?"

"If that's how you want to put it."

The conversation again fell into a deep well that would have allowed him to say, "Okay, thanks for calling, good night." But there were too many worlds that had been unlocked, and Loriano was surprised to find that he felt a need for two minutes longer. Apart from sleep, he wasn't missing anything else. "Nives, do you know what I was thinking?"

"What?"

"Donatella is my Rosa. At least, she's one of the ghosts I see."

"I told you, she gives you a wide berth."

He sighed. "She's a stupid old thing," he said to himself. But he didn't waste the momentum of that wave of melancholy that had unexpectedly washed over him, in his dressing gown by the telephone table. "She broke after Amedeo. She made all these scenes about her weight . . . she had it in for me, too. Maybe that's when I took to the bottle."

"That's when the vendetta started."

"I feel like I'm talking to the wall."

"What?"

"Nothing."

"Just had to blow off steam sometimes. I remember it as if it were yesterday."

"Donatella?"

"No, Renato. You should have seen him: with no shirt on, down the gully on the banks of the stream, in the middle of July, the crickets humming around him. He was like a bronze statue."

Bottai put a stop to the cloud-burst of emotions. In Nives' place, he pictured his wife when she was a girl, about to put her panties back on. He would never have thought it, but all of a sudden, he felt jealous, just like that, on a random Tuesday night. He felt a wave of resentment; and yet, he rather enjoyed diving back into the assortment of surprises Nives had served up. "What did he say?"

"Rosaltea wouldn't let him go. She would follow him around. He would bump into her everywhere. She sent him letters that he never even read. One afternoon, after we'd done it, he said, 'She might be here right now.' My breasts were still bare. A shiver came over me. After that, something changed. It was hard to refuse Renato. Once you'd unstopped that bottle, there was only one thing on your mind—you don't find wine like that in every cellar. Minutes after quashing a glass, you want another flask of the stuff, if you get my meaning."

"I get your meaning alright, Nives. I get your meaning."

"Anyway, the idea of being spied on by a love-sick crazy

woman poisoned us. It wasn't enough to change our assignations. Whether we were at the gully, or at the end of an alleyway, Rosa's dark eyes were a constant presence. Maybe Renato liked the feeling of being watched. He was a talented lover, and had quite a few little fixations. If a girl fell into his hands, there was no way to resist him. And we girls were hungry for knowledge then . . ."

"Please go on."

"At one point, she was always number two on our list of things to talk about. Number one was the games we'd gotten up to, and then we'd always end up talking about Rosaltea. The madwoman had started targeting us, too. Donatella was particularly shocked by her spiteful pranks."

"We're still taking about *my* Donatella, right?"

"Who else?"

Loriano sighed. "Who else, indeed."

"We found little dishes by our front doors."

"Little dishes?"

"Little dishes of piss."

"I don't know anything about this."

"And braided string on our windowsills, with stones tied up inside."

"It sounds like witchcraft."

"Demaria had a cold that lasted all winter."

"That can happen with the change of season."

"She coughed up phlegm for months."

"In those days, you were sick for much longer."

"Tucci, on the other hand, started itching. First her elbows, then behind her ears. She scratched her skin until it bled."

"It's called psoriasis. It's usually stress that causes it."

"Donatella was the worst off."

"*My* Donatella?"

"Her pussy smelled like a dead body."

"What?"

"She couldn't get rid of the stench. It made you retch from twenty yards away. She walked into a store and everyone ran a mile. She got to the point that she never went out."

Loriano glanced at the bedroom again. That was why he'd never heard about her youthful experiences: they'd ended with the shame of vaginal infections. He forgave his wife everything, if there was something to forgive. "Didn't anything happen to you?" he asked with a hint of irony.

"I stopped sleeping."

"That's still a problem now, I hear."

"After a week without any sleep, I couldn't even remember my home address. Mom sent me to bed with giant cups of chamomile and valerian tea, but it didn't help."

"The power of suggestion can play nasty tricks."

Nives spoke as if she were reliving her past. "One of us with distemper and another with lesions. Donatella shut in her room, branded by the stench of a carcass. Then there was me, reduced to a shadow of myself."

"A lovely invasion of bacteria, viruses, and other disturbances."

"It was clear to us that it was a curse. Messing around with Renato had been fun, but afterwards even hearing his name gave us goosebumps.

"Better late than never."

"One morning, they took Frida Bonelli to the hospital. We heard that she'd started having massive nose bleeds.

After soaking a bed sheet, there seemed to be no way to stem the flow . . . she calmed down, too. Soon after, she decided to toe the line, and she only had eyes for her husband after that."

"The germs were spread around the group. Together with the paranoia."

"For Renato, it made no difference; he went and looked elsewhere. He'd already started hanging out in the city."

"I remember him then. We sometimes met on the bus. I was loaded with books, and he was wearing this leather bomber jacket, like a US Air Force pilot. I really wanted one, but they were so expensive. We traveled together, me furiously taking notes and him staring out the window."

"He'd already started."

"To do what?"

"He used to go and see sprightly old ladies."

"Ah, you mean that."

"Yes, that. He would vanish from Monday to Saturday. Some wives went mad waiting for him, but the curse had already calmed the ardors of most of them. The hard part was staying firm when he was right there within slapping distance of you. He'd fix you with those green eyes, and you were already wet."

"He used to go to his workshop."

"What?"

"He liked painting. He told me about an artist that had taken a shine to him. He became his assistant. And learned something meanwhile."

"Yes, it was his thing at the time. He'd go around with that worn-out pencil case, filled with charcoal and wax crayons. One thing that made you fall in love with him was that, after having sex, he'd draw you. You'd let him do it.

You'd let that guy do anything. He'd spread your hair out on the grass and you'd lie there, naked, with his eyes on you. It was like giving yourself to him all over again. If anyone wanted to find out how many girls Renato Pagliuchi had laid, all they'd need to do is leaf through his sketchbooks, where he practiced his drawing skills. You'd have it dripping down your thighs, and there he was dipping in to you with another kind of brush. It penetrated you just as much. Maybe more."

For Loriano, the conversation was like navigating a minefield. With every word an image of Donatella with no clothes on, dripping wet between her legs, could blow up in his face. "Maestro," he said, to shake himself free of the image. "That's what he used to call him."

"Who?"

"The painter there. The one who had a workshop. Renato used to call him Maestro."

"They were lovers."

"Nives, what are you talking—"

"Edoardo Giambattista Freschi-Valeri."

"You need a day's vacation just to say his name."

"They were lovers."

"Well, that's the kind of nonsense I don't want to hear. This is worse than Rosa rising from the dead to kill you when you're at the end of your life anyway."

"He was his model."

"That's another matter altogether."

"He used to draw naked Christ figures."

"Christ?"

"Naked."

"But they were actually—"

"If you go and look at the man's paintings from that

period, you'll see many portraits of Renato Pagliuchi. His face. His body. Even the moles are the same. In our town and in the city, there's one in nearly every house. Women throughout the province liked having an Adonis to look at whenever they wanted. Right out there in the open, with their husbands reading the papers in an armchair beside them."

Bottai made a mental search of the house: there were no paintings of crucifixions or anything at home. He breathed a sigh of relief. He was surprised to find that he was intrigued. The secret life of his long-time friend was coming out. "At the time, he was famous for his womanizing and for getting beaten up now and again by jealous beaus. He'd walk into the local café with a black eye and split lip: people envied him his trophies. Knowing that he's been immortalized in the role of Jesus Christ makes me think fondly of him. It's one way to run a workshop."

"The painter paid his gorgeous pupil with an apprenticeship."

"When you're rich, you always find a way not to open up your purse strings."

"Another thing was that most of his bruises were not inflicted by betrayed partners."

"Who was it then?"

"His father."

"You mean old Bardo?"

"Yes, him. He's a piece of shit."

"With us kids he was always friendly. He used to give us cigarettes. He'd sometimes buy us sweets, too."

"In the evenings, he'd hand out more to his son, with the back of his hand."

Bottai stopped and thought for a moment. He wondered

what it was that had upset the father: he had a son who was built like a statue and who pulled in girls from morning to night. For a father of that ilk, his son's triumphs were proof of good blood, as if he himself had conquered the girls and married women. "What was he upset about?"

"The painting, for example. If it wasn't house-painting or whitewashing cellars, it reeked of a pastime for faggots, if you get my meaning."

Loriano shook his head. "Bardo was more sophisticated than that."

"In front of others, he played the part of the friend everyone would wish for. Inside the four walls of his house, though, he took his son and nailed him down. Take work, for example. There was no way he was going to send him to art school. There wasn't much money around. Renato couldn't accept it. He wanted to take up the palette. He'd come over the ridge and down to the river with his face smashed in, and guess what?"

"Let's hear it."

"We fell even more deeply in love. We turned into the little nurses from the Red Cross that he'd always been looking for. If it weren't blasphemous, I'd say that he was even better looking when he'd been beaten up. Those fleshy lips, split by his father's beatings. When he laughed, they'd open and bleed."

"So, there's the explanation for the epidemic."

"Bardo was a bad drinker. Outside the house, he was everyone's friend; inside, he dictated the law, like a drunken old Fascist. When Renato got to the gully with his face smashed in, there were those of us who crossed ourselves because we didn't have much time and we didn't want to waste any of it listening to his complaints. Unlike them, I liked listening. Maybe more than stripping off for him . . . Well, no, not that much."

Loriano felt deeply resentful on his friend's behalf. "You used him."

"Just as he used us."

"He was looking for refuge. More for his soul than for his desires, it seems to me."

"He found that in me. Not in the others."

Attempting to wrap things up, Bottai said, "In any case, he didn't become a painter. In the end, he was a bus driver, on the same route where I used to see him, early in the morning wearing that aviator's jacket."

"That's his Rosa."

Loriano sighed. "Right."

"And then the painter was found dead."

"What?"

"Surrounded by paintings in his studio. With a knife stuck into his belly."

"I never heard about that."

"The news was a bombshell, but in our little town who cares about artist types? Demaria saw it in the newspaper. She summoned us all one day, her eyes out of their orbits.

"To do what?"

"We didn't say anything to begin with. We were scared of getting involved in something crazy like that. It was Tucci who put our suspicions into words. "Do you think it was Rosaltea?"

"Oh, do me a favor!"

"That was my reaction, too. Blaming her for the curse was one thing, but this was a much more delicate matter."

"I know." Bottai's stomach clenched at the idea that

the accusation had been bandied about. It sullied her memory.

"You know Donatella. She's not scared of anything. 'She wants him to herself,' she declared. Demaria notched things up further. 'His visits to the painter were convincing him to leave home and vanish into the big city.' It was my turn to put the cherry on the cake, but I said it without thinking, as a joke. 'If anything, the fact that he's naked in that man's paintings might not sit well with her. If she's gone soft in the head, why not completely soft?'"

"You must have been so bored."

"In the streets, we'd exchanged furtive looks with the wives we knew had had dealings with the town toy boy. We said 'good morning' to them through pursed lips. Meaning: 'Look out!'"

Loriano chuckled. "That was over the top."

"Anyway, it was a tough blow for Renato. After being interrogated, he stopped going into the city. One evening, Bardo told him what he thought in no uncertain terms: 'Look where your mania for stupid drawings has gotten you.' He went around looking grim. He took to the bottle a little more than he should have, which he'd always avoided before, seeing how you lot were wrecking yourselves, wasting your evenings at the local bar. Renato tried going back to his old ways a few times, trying to shake himself out of it. 'Shall we go and do some sketches?' That's what he'd say, but even the ugly girls would reject him."

"Did they ever find him?"

"Who?"

"The one who stuck the knife in."

"They said it was bad debts or something like that."

"I bet there wasn't even a name or a face attached."

"Exactly."

"So, you all got stuck on the idea that it was Rosa."

"There's no other explanation."

"It was the most logical answer," Bottai said, sarcastically.

"Nobody would ever have suspected her."

"Except you girls."

"Except us girls."

"And Renato."

"It was different for him."

"Why?"

He took her for granted. There were lots of girls with crushes on him. He treated Rosa like he treated the others, ignoring them and making them die of desire. He loved being courted. She wasn't that stupid. She went on following him around, but she'd learned not to be caught out. As far as Renato was concerned, she was one of the many girls who'd given up on him after a fling. Like hell she was."

"How do you know?"

"Easy. We followed her."

Loriano rubbed his eyes. "Rosaltea followed Renato, and you followed Rosaltea?"

"She might have killed the painter."

"Was Donatella with this gang of idiots?"

"After lashings of mint tincture, she managed to cure the disease in her panties, but she was the most anxious of us all. She was devoured by an obsession. She always had to know where Rosaltea was, otherwise she'd be convinced she was standing right behind her. So, she started tracking her every move. But it was never enough for Donatella. To keep her cool, she would have had to pin Rosaltea's shadow to her, even when she went to the bathroom."

He glanced back towards the bedroom. "Crazy."

"She had two lives. One normal, all smiles and smooth-talking. The other, in the shadows.

"Rosa, you mean?"

"Yes, Rosa."

"She was a waitress at Momo's."

"As soon as she took her apron off, she was something else."

"Heads turned when she served the tables."

"Her face was nondescript."

"Her smile was enough to wake the dead."

"We took turns."

"Turns?"

"Some of us were studying at the time. Tucci and Demaria, for example. I was an apprentice at the Fracassi cleaning company, working part-time."

"The great Taddeo Fracassi!"

"Donatella was the best-off; she was already pulling down a full salary."

"She still takes out the tools of her trade sometimes and goes to see clients at home; people who trust her and nobody else. Those are the good days. On those evenings, she sits down to dinner more grounded."

"Working with a family firm gave her a lot of freedom."

"And she wasted it running after that poor wretch?"

"In the end, most of us ran out of steam. All the intrigue at the beginning was soon forgotten. At that age, things move along quickly. In my case, for example, I'd set my eyes on that hunk who came into town on Sundays from the countryside."

"Poor Anteo."

"We gradually stopped wasting our time. Whether or not it was Rosaltea, the painter was six feet under. We'd played a bit-part in a mystery for a while, but that was it."

"Well put."

"Instead, Donatella couldn't make peace with it. She would arrive with detailed reports. Since she was so keen on tailing the girl for hours, we let her do it. We listened, as we would a radio drama. Then she found something out."

"What?"

"Rosa had a boyfriend."

"There you go!"

"They'd meet on Wednesdays, late at night. Down at the soccer fields. Right by the restaurant. Rather than go home after her shift, she'd go the other way. Think about it. Wednesdays, low season. If there were three tables a night at Momo's it was a miracle. Just like now."

"That's proof, then."

"Proof of what?"

"She had other affairs. Being discarded like an old glove by the boy she was in love with was painful, but she'd gotten over it. She was moving on. Curses and these terrible suspicions of yours had nothing to do with it."

"It was Bardo."

"Who?"

"Rosa's boyfriend."

Loriano had to steady himself by leaning on the telephone table. "What are you saying?"

"It was him."

"Nives, these are things that—"

"Since she couldn't have the son, she had the father. In

secret. It was all in the family, after all. There was a bit of Renato for her there!"

"I don't believe it."

"I'm not making it up."

"You must have seen wrong."

"We saw what we saw."

"These are unpleasant accusations."

"Bardo was the beast here. He must have been nearly fifty at the time, and he couldn't have believed his own luck when he got his hands on a girl who was only just eighteen."

"As far as I know, he's still in a care home."

"He must be a hundred by now . . . they used to meet down at the playing fields and do what they were there to do. As soon as they started, we left, with shivers running up our spines. Bardo looked like an old, decrepit man to us."

"What a story."

"Rosaltea had everything twisted up."

"Did she go on chasing Pagliuchi?"

"Whenever she had a free moment, that's who she'd be thinking about."

"I can't remember any of it. Renato was one of us. He'd join us when we went out on the town, especially after we first got our driving licenses. He was always happy to tag along, even though quite a few of the gang turned their noses up when they saw he was coming. He was a few years younger than us. But that wasn't why. We'd walk onto the dance floor, and all the girls' eyes were on him. Followed by the eyes of the boyfriends and envious suitors. A brawl would break out over nothing. It was part of the fun, in the end. He never turned away from a fight, no sir. Sometimes he comes downstairs to try out the grappa, and we talk about the old times!"

"What does Donatella say?"

"She usually hides away in the sitting room in front of the TV."

"She's ashamed."

"I don't think so. She's just not interested in hearing about all the pranks we got up to when we were kids. She prefers her TV series."

"She was the one who was most into it."

"Into what?"

"Mysteries. Intrigues like that."

"She's never mentioned any of this since the day I first met her. Does that seem normal to you?"

"She's ashamed."

"Did you tell poor Anteo everything?"

"God, no."

"Never? Not even about the curse?"

"God, no."

"And then you go and tittle-tattle to me about my own wife. I can't work out whether you're trying to stir up trouble, or what you're up to."

"We fell into the subject. One word leads to another, and here we are. I want to see you happy, believe me."

"That may well be . . . but let's get back to the point. You were talking about a girl who was into it."

Nives took a moment to get back into her story. "Once she found out about the secret assignations at the playing fields, Donatella started chewing over it in her head. After a while, she reached her verdict. She spat it out, just like that, with no embellishments."

"Let's hear it."

"In her view, it was Bardo who'd stabbed the painter."

"She was a thinker, alright."

"She said it was not completely unlikely that Renato's father had found out about his affair with the artist."

"Which still needs to be proved, by the way."

"How am I supposed to know? There were a few lines written on a scrap of paper . . . One thing is sure: Bardo would have accepted anything but having a fag for a son. That it would have gutted him is an understatement."

Loriano thought for a minute. He had to admit Nives was right. Pagliuchi Sr. was the kind of man who could easily have punished an offence committed by his own flesh and blood with more blood. He could be as friendly as anything, but he flew into a rage over nothing. He was a man from another era. One thing that had always shocked him was how Renato's father would deal with the hunting dogs he wasn't happy with. He could still hear Bardo's gruff voice. Sitting on the café bench, he'd say, "I'm not wasting a bullet on you," and drag the poor, inadequate creatures out into the scrub. He'd entice them with dog biscuits in his hand. He'd let the animals smell them in one hand while, with the other, he'd slit their jugulars with a blade and then eat the biscuits himself. Loriano trembled at the memory. "These accusations are serious."

"He could have shut Rosa up the same way."

"Really? You're veering towards science fiction now."

"Think about it. Maybe she knew about Renato's affair with the artist. She might have been blackmailing her handsome playboy. In any case, the situation is proof enough: Bardo uses her a few times and then decides to end it. Too risky. A scandal of the kind could break up more than one family."

"Rosaltea jumped from the belfry in front of the whole town."

"Wrong."

"For God's sake, I was there!"

"You heard the thud."

"What more do we need to know?"

"How did she get into the church? How come nobody saw her? You said something before that scared me, but it also switched a lightbulb on in my mind."

"What am I supposed to have said?"

"She was in her nightie."

"It's the truth," Bottai stammered. "I was there. I saw her."

"And she was barefoot?"

"Exactly."

"A girl crosses town, from her house to the church. That's at least a five-minute walk. In a nightie. Barefoot. And nobody speaks to her?"

"Well."

"You said something else."

"What?"

"The market stalls."

"So?"

"The market stalls were out."

"Yes, I'm sure about that."

"So, it was market day," she went on.

"If there were market stalls."

"Which means it was Thursday."

"As per usual."

"What does that make you think?"

"What does it make me think?"

"The next day."

"Nives, you're doing my head in."

"When did they use to meet at the playing fields?"

"Wednesdays, late."

"And when did she jump from the belfry?"

Loriano was forced to admit it. "Thursday morning."

"A few hours later. Could that be chance?"

"Of course."

"There's more."

"You're worse than Lieutenant Columbo."

"There was no scream. That's what you said, right?"

Bottai caught a glimpse of himself sitting at the outdoor table, lost in a conversation with poor old Tancredi. That old friend of his always managed to coax a laugh out of him, whatever he said . . . the dull thud. "I could swear it in front of a judge. Not a sound."

"That's not normal. Jumping from a height like that, you'd let out a scream instinctively."

"Fear could have taken her breath away. Or maybe she was simply not herself."

"I'm just saying this, okay? Are we really sure that Rosa died and went to heaven when she landed on the cobblestones? Or was she put to sleep before? She was a wisp of a girl remember."

"Yes, but not so small you could put her in your pocket."

"What's true is that the business with the nightie has put a bee in my bonnet."

Bottai felt a little foolish, but he gave the idea some consideration nevertheless. "Kidnapping her in her sleep, giving her a knock on the head, and carrying her up to the top of the bell tower sounds a bit far-fetched when you think that she used to choose the empty alleys to scurry around in because they were steeper and full of steps. She managed to creep into the church without being seen because everyone was busy buying eggplant. She reached the top of the tower and killed herself. End of story."

"Which alleys are you talking about?"

"How do I know? The back lanes that make old people's hips ache. They're always deserted. Only stray cats go up and down them. I was just thinking out loud, Nives. Stop weighing every word I say."

"It would work, though."

"Pity it's just the idle chat of two insomniacs who have given up on the idea of going to sleep."

"It would work though."

"You're saying I'm right, then?"

"Not at all. Bardo grabs her, takes the deserted back lanes, and throws her off the tower."

Loriano broke away from the yarn with a sigh. "I'm tired now." His brain had truly turned to pulp.

"You're as cold as a stone. Doesn't anything shock you?"

He shrugged. "What are we supposed to do? Go and knock on the door of the police station and feed them all this swill? What for? To lock up old Bardo who can hardly remember what he ate for breakfast? They'll end up leading us away in a straitjacket."

"She's asking us to do it."

"Who?"

"Rosaltea. She's yelling her curse at us, so that the truth will come out, and she can finally rest in peace."

"Nives, solitude is not doing you any favors."

"I've never been more awake than now."

Loriano glanced at the clock. "Same here."

"Look at all it took to get to this point: Anteo dead and buried, a farm animal for company."

"I'd forgotten about the hen." Bottai glimpsed an opportunity to break off the conversation. "Is she still asleep?"

Nives looked into the living room. "Mother Mary, the shivers!"

"What's she doing?"

"She's still there on the armchair, as still as a statue. Do you think she's possessed? Rosaltea must have turned her to stone to make me pick up the phone and call you—"

"Who's ever heard of a ghost possessing a hen? Anyway, she can't talk."

"They are pure creatures. Getting under the skin of a human is much more complicated."

"Now you're a witch, too."

"Nonna Landa used to know stuff. Farm workers would bring her half a shoulder of ham in exchange for predicting the movements of the earth with her pendulum. I know stuff, too."

"Spirits inhabiting hens."

"They're in the cats, too."

"And the pheasants?"

"Don't be a fool. One time they brought in a girl who was as pretty as a picture. She'd woken up to find a viper under her pillow. Her hair started to fall out that same day. Her name was Zaira."

"A terrible shock can do worse."

"No, it was the evil eye. Nonna Landa mixed up one of her potions, and then she gave the girl a duck's neck."

"A duck's neck?"

"To keep on the bedsprings under her mattress."

"Do me a favor—"

"She had to keep it there from new moon to new moon."

"Imagine the stench."

"Actually, Zaira stopped losing patches of hair. My dear old fox, these things happen."

Loriano felt an unexpected stab of tenderness. It was the first time that his old friend had confided in him this way, revealing the ignorance of her peasant roots. Ultimately, it cost him nothing to let her believe in fortune-tellers and potions, the dead speaking through owls, or magic stones. May everyone choose their own solitude. Finding an explanation, even if it is crazy, keeps you company. Bottai steered the conversation back. "Give her a blow."

"Sorry?"

"Pick the creature up and blow on her beak."

"How do you mean?"

"I saw it in a magic show once. There was a dove. The magician hypnotized it and then blew on its beak to wake it up again."

Nives thought for a moment. "No, the idea gives me the creeps."

"But you tuck her in like a baby! From what you said, I wouldn't be surprised if you wiped her private parts clean before going to bed . . . so, what's wrong with a blow?"

"She might get a fright, not recognize me, and peck my nose off."

Loriano rolled his eyes. "You're always imagining what might happen. You can't go on like this."

"Focus on your own household. I know how to hold my own here, you know."

Bottai shook his head. He would happily have opened a debate on the beliefs of country folk, who were sure they knew everything without ever venturing beyond the road sign marking the provincial boundary. Every day he had to fight with them when they held onto their cheap theories as if they were well-founded principles. Maybe that was why he needed two bottles of wine a day, one for each meal. He decided, at that time of night, that he really didn't have the strength to engage in an in-depth conversation of the kind. "Try a hair-dryer; that might do it," he said.

"A hair-dryer?"

"Try it."

"What if I dry her eyes out? She's already half-crazed as it is."

"Wring her neck," Loriano thought to himself, exasperated by her theatrics. "And then kill yourself, too." His tongue grated on his palate, forming words that were not that different, in the end. "I don't know what else to suggest."

"Quite the luminary!"

"For sure, books don't teach you to wake sleep-walking animals. Science has different priorities."

"So do some doctors. Especially if you put a flask of wine on the table."

In his mind, Bottai abandoned the match. While, until that moment, one of his aims had been to help his friend wake the hen up to prove that there was no ghost involved, now he surrendered. It was time to stop going on about his drinking. He had a certain weakness. He found a certain comfort in it. He didn't like the idea that every glass he drank would be poisoned by the words of a mad old widow. He answered brusquely, "Nives, it's gotten really late."

"That's what you always used to say."

"What?"

"You heard me."

Loriano felt an unexpected lurch. "What are you talking about now?"

"You know."

He looked towards the bedroom, alarmed, as if Nives had spoken those words into a megaphone. She went on the attack. "Are you senile and a drunk?"

"Nives—"

"Don't worry, I was joking."

"I'm in fits."

"Oh, get over it. We're two old things, always happy to talk about old times. In any case, I'm the one paying for the phone call. Stop huffing and puffing as though someone was pulling out your lungs."

Loriano felt the crazy woman had his back against the wall. She was going completely off track, bringing up things from a hundred lifetimes ago. His heart started beating wildly. Before speaking, he put a hand over the receiver as if it were a shield. "What am I supposed to say?"

"For example, that you were a handsome young fellow."

"I knew it. I should have hung up immediately. All those stories about Rosaltea, Pagliuchi, Donatella . . . The whole thing with the hen is a lie, right?"

"Ugh, you give yourself such airs. You haven't changed one bit."

"So, what are you looking for, exactly? Listen. Let's do

each other a favor. Hang up and no hard feelings; friends like before."

"To be your friend, I'd have to be born all over again. Possibly in the middle of China. But anyway, even the walls know: no matter the country, you'll always find a Bottai."

"We're not doing each other any favors."

Nives was pleased by the agitated tone of his voice. She felt as though she had a diminutive Loriano Bottai in her clutches. "To tell the truth, you wrapped up your horrible gift with your own hands, back in the day. Without even attaching a label."

"What's the point of bringing this up now?"

"What's the point of never talking about it?"

Bottai felt his chest tightening. "The past is full of ghosts. For all of us. That's how it is, and that's how it will always be. Talking tonight, thirty years later, will serve no purpose."

"Look at Rosaltea."

"Not her again."

"Speaking of ghosts that are unable to find peace."

"You and I are alive and kicking."

"Speak for yourself. A certain Nives was massacred back in '82. What happened afterwards is another matter. It's not easy living with the ghost of what you could have been. You look in the mirror and, before you have time to say good morning, that's what you see."

"Don't exaggerate. And how would a little chat now change anything?"

"At least you're keeping me company. Given that you didn't have the courage for all the rest."

"You're talking as if I'd hurt you on purpose."

"I'm talking about it because I feel like I've been cheated."

"It's because of Anteo. A death like that would throw anyone."

"Don't you dare mention him now. Not in this conversation."

"You're attacking me for nothing. He was a friend. He still would be if—"

"Back in the cane thicket, you felt differently."

Loriano jumped. He belted his words into the receiver, "Nives, are you crazy?"

"I have been, for sure."

He tried to hold himself back. "I know what you're after."

"Bottai understands something for once. We should put it in the calendar."

When Loriano spoke, it was as if his tongue had been dipped in poison. "You are on your own. Seeing as you're not doing too well, you can't stand that things have gone differently for others. Your only dream is to see the world going to pot. You stick your arm into the past, right up to your armpits, and you love stirring the dirty water you find there. You're even bringing Rosaltea into it, poor girl. You're sprinkling pepper all over a Donatella who was so young at the time that milk still dribbled from her mouth."

"Well, what Pagliuchi dispensed was more like *stracciatella* than milk."

Bottai didn't fall for it. "This whole tsunami you've brought on one random evening with the excuse of a half-crazed hen! What's it for? What's your purpose? The answer is sadly pathetic."

"I'm curious."

Loriano took his time. He knew that he'd launched a cavalcade that wouldn't necessarily lead him to victory; he needed to pull on the reins a little. He paused for a while. Then, very calmly, he said, "Nives, there's no point in trying to wreck my marriage. There's nothing in it for you."

More silence. Broken by a loud, throaty laugh. Bottai held the receiver to his chest. He felt a tickling sensation, right against his heart. It lasted at least half a minute. As soon as he thought it was over, he held it up again to his ear. "Are you done?"

"Imbecile!"

"It's what I think. You know I'm right."

Nives was surprisingly offended. All of a sudden, she saw herself as an old woman begging for crumbs. Before fully appreciating what that meant, she heard herself say, "I don't need to inconvenience that steam train you keep in your bed." She regretted it immediately because by uttering these words, she was proving Loriano right. She was almost pleased.

"If that's all, I'd say we could bring this to an end. Thanks for calling."

"Sometimes I look at the old photos."

"Which photos?"

"There's one at the fall fair with me, you, and Donatella . . . Anteo had just won a racing bike at the charity raffle. I'm wearing a lovely white dress, with red and blue flowers. You can't see the colors anymore."

"I remember that dress."

"We're sitting at a long table. If you count all the heads, there are twenty-two of us."

"They were great, those evenings."

"You're looking at me."

". . ."

"I'm looking at you."

". . ."

"The heavens could have exploded over our heads: we'd already decided."

"Nives, this isn't good for me."

"My bag was already packed. I'd stowed it under the same bed I sleep in now. I'd only taken a few things . . . they were weeks of hell. In the bathroom in the evenings, I'd take my wedding ring off and put it on the hand basin. I'd gaze at that naked hand. I'd sometimes feel a little dizzy: would I really be able to carry it through? The answer was always loud and clear. There was no other option: I had to do it. Period. After the partying at the fall fair, it was a miracle we got home. Anteo drove with only one eye open, he'd drunk so much wine and spirits. It would have been a real pity to crash on a curve. Maybe I shouldn't say this, but on a thousand different occasions I found myself wishing we had done so, thinking, 'If only he'd died that night!' I've already told you that something died that October 13, '82. I stripped my husband and put him to bed. He fell asleep on the spot. I looked at him for a long time, as if I were waiting for a divine voice to order me to stop, to clear my head of that madness. It never came. So, I pulled my ring off for the last time and put it on the bedside table. I hauled my bag out from under the bed. As I closed the door behind me, I had to fight the worst battle. Leaving home knowing you'll never come back is a strange feeling. I left my set of keys in the lock. Walking down the track, I didn't look back once. Until I reached the asphalt. It was midnight. The moon was waning. I had to hold myself together with all my strength. Every now and again, a mild gust of wind shook the leaves. Every time, I thought I could hear an engine revving. And I said to myself, 'Here he is! Here he is! We're actually doing this.' I looked at the curve of the road. I was so out of it that I was sure the headlights of a car were illuminating it. But they never came. When I got back home, I was a piece of marble. I put my key-chain back in its place and my bag back under the bed. Anteo hadn't budged an inch. I put my ring back on. As I pushed it down my finger, I thought I could hear the clinking of metal, like handcuffs. I went to the bathroom and wiped away the little makeup that was left on my face. I undressed and put on my same old nightie. As I lay under the covers, I felt grief well up inside me. It never left."

Too many words. Too heavy with meaning. Loriano stood there at the telephone table, staring into space. It was as if somebody had surprised him from behind and planted a knife in his back.

Nives was not doing too well either. She went on. "That evening, you left me at Poggio Corbello. Thirty years later, I'm still here, as frozen as the hen in my living room. You should know how to snap her out of it, but as usual you're useless."

Bottai had to make a huge effort to break out of the iron mask he felt trapped in. He uttered words that, in any other circumstance, would have sounded hopeful, but which fell out of his mouth like rocks. "There was Amedeo."

It was a sensitive point. Nives felt herself burn inside. "You couldn't have known that." She knew as soon as it came out that it was a terrible thing to say. But it was too late.

Loriano looked towards the bedroom. "Donatella's period was late."

The months and years following that October night rushed through Nives's mind. Everything was over with Loriano. There had been no need to talk about it. As if a wicked spell had been cast, they were transformed from undying lovers filled with promises into acquaintances who had always been in full view. She decided to exact her revenge. "A few days later, the same thing happened to me."

"What?"

"I was late."

Bottai breathed a sigh of relief. He had regained control. His tone changed accordingly. "Sometimes life responds like that, with plain facts. '82 was fine where we'd left it, without wrecking two families and the lives of two little kids."

"You wanted to marry me." Nives had to make an effort not to say, "You *should* have." "You were fixated with America. You left that by the side of the road, at the crossroads with me."

This was a slap in the face for Loriano. He looked away from the point he'd been staring at, as if he were avoiding her eyes. "If we were to count all the stupid things we say . . ."

"Stupid things?"

"We say a lot of them, especially at that age."

"In that regard, you were king."

"But I really believed it. I didn't say it to hurt you."

"But you did."

"I hurt myself first."

"And me second."

"And yet—"

"Laura third."

Loriano had to think hard to put a face to the name. "Laura?"

"Haven't you ever noticed?"

"Laura?"

"She has the same initial as you. Her name isn't that far off from yours."

Standing at the telephone table, Loriano had a waking dream: that he could be cleaved in two, so that he wouldn't have to find out anything more about anything. In the meantime, Nives had grabbed her battle-ax. Considering their exchange, there was nothing she wanted more than to wield it in order to reduce certain facts to pulp. And shed buckets of blood. "That was how I cried 'us' for a whole lifetime: with my daughter's name," she said.

Loriano was losing his mind; a lightning storm flashed a thousand images of him, moment by moment. Him sitting at the café while Nives walks past pushing a stroller, barely saying "good morning." Him at the school gates, on those rare days when work allowed him to pick up Amedeo. Nives there for her little girl not even glancing at him. Him with a drink (so many glasses; an infinite number of glasses) until, at a certain point in his inebriation, he was sucked back into the same old sink-hole: an image of a beautiful young woman, at night, left standing on the side of the road like one of the old whores from Collacchie. Him up at Poggio Corbello with his friend Anteo, on an urgent call to check the rabbits, mostly to exclude an outbreak of ringworm. An invitation into the kitchen for a drop of grappa, seeing a young girl intent on watching the cartoons. Nives bustling around them as if they were friends again. All this and more was reduced to three precise words, "Is she mine?"

"Whatever, she's grown up fine. She finished high school and lives in France now. She gave us two grandchildren whose names I can hardly pronounce."

Bottai's throat was dry. The urge to rush to the other room and grab a bottle by the neck was overwhelming, but from one moment to the next, his confusion turned into rage. "And this is how you tell me?"

"I can't do it in French."

Loriano felt as though the floor was rising all of a sudden. In his mind, the version of the story he had always told himself was that two little offspring had magically appeared in order to clarify the situation and stop living as if they were split in two—a sign from the Gods that they had invoked for weeks, indicating the right path to take. To begin with, it had been strange to see Donatella and Nives both pregnant—for a while he'd even hated Nives (anger is important fuel for ending an ill-fated love affair): despite their affair, she'd been sleeping with her husband and was parading the fact around in those loose clothes that announced a happy event; the same loose clothes his wife wore, which in turn revealed the games he'd been playing— but it is a well-known fact that a man who doesn't pay his dues in bed is the first to raise the alarm. In sum, Bottai had played the stallion for everyone's good. Including Anteo's. Armed with this latest development and all his past woes, he spat the words out without any preamble. "You bitch!"

Nives flinched. "Excuse me?"

"I was right. Now that Anteo is dead, you've come here to present me with the bill, thirty years after the fact. This little amusement will come back to haunt you: it'll be the end of Donatella, and you'll ruin my Amedeo, along with his wife and kids. And Laura's fate won't be any better. Her father fresh in the grave until she finds out he's alive and well, with another name." Loriano couldn't stop himself from adding, "Anyway, who says she's mine? It sounds like the delusion of a widow who talks to her hens."

Nives was so still, she didn't even blink. In the silence that followed, Bottai was on tenterhooks, ready for whatever came next, anything from the wildest of curses to more unhinged laughter. He imagined her hanging up on him and then coming to ring on his doorbell at midnight, an old flame ready to send his world to rack and ruin, even dragging old Pagliuchi downstairs from his attic apartment. He saw himself getting a hotel room, like those disastrous men who wreck their families after thirty years because they indulged too cavalierly in a fling. Except, in his case, he was hurtling headlong toward seventy, with everything that entails. Including the rapid darkening of his horizons. Including the fact that, at a certain age, solitude can terrify you . . . Instead, she resolved everything with two matter-of-fact words, uttered almost sleepily, "Anteo knew."

This time it was Loriano who laughed jeeringly. "Tell me another one."

Despite his protests, Nives suddenly felt calm. As serene, perhaps, as she had been for a long time. "In the early days, I dreamed about it," she said. "You'd bought that Alfetta, which looked like it belonged to some sleazy, wannabe cop. Everyone envied you. It was nothing like the Fiat 127 you had before, which was always full of straw and clumps of earth so that, whenever I got home, I'd find a bruise in some odd place or other . . . I was in my third month when I saw you racing by in your flashy new car. It felt like having my teeth smashed. 'Loriano has erased me.' That's what I thought. But then I started dreaming about it."

"About what?"

"Us driving really fast down a road. On one side, mountains; on the other, the sea. It was in France. We wouldn't say a word to one another, but there was always one moment when you'd turn and look at me. We were totally inebriated with the craziness of what we'd just done, with so many miles still to go before we got to America. Try and imagine how I felt when Laura came and told me a few years ago that she'd set her sights on this young, foreign man. Sometimes the signs fell like torrential rain on a sunny day. This is all to say that there is no way they'll ever see me go and visit them in those places. I dreamed about France in a certain way, and that's enough for me."

Loriano was trying to hold up, despite the most colossal hangover he'd ever had. He felt duty-bound to say something, but nothing came out. Nives went on. "As soon as I opened my eyes, I felt two kicks to my stomach. One was realizing I was still in the same old bed; the other was realizing I was going to have your daughter. She had been abandoned at the turnoff to the big road, like me. Sometimes, Anteo would find me in floods of tears before it was even time for my *latte* at breakfast. I blamed it on the pregnancy."

"How did he know?"

"He spent his life in the fields, but he wasn't stupid."

"Nobody ever thought he was."

"Laura was nine years old when I found a piece of paper."

"What piece of paper?"

"He'd gotten himself tested. The results were clear; even I could understand them. His sperm-count was close to zero. Maybe the little tadpoles had been killed off by the mild bout of meningitis he'd had as a kid . . ."

Loriano took this shot, too. Life's truly a bitch, when it decides to be, he thought. He went over the thousands of moments he'd spent with his friend. Discovering that Anteo had carried such a heavy secret made him reinterpret every single greeting they'd ever exchanged through the years, from when they shared a desk at school to when they shared a drink at the bar, and finally to when they'd had their last Stravecchio together. His breath caught in his throat. "Nives, are you done with your revelations?"

"Are you complaining? What about the poor man who brought up a girl her whole life without saying a word? Worse. When you were called in to tend to one of the animals, you'd even get a tip for your troubles. Just so you understand what kind of stuff a man worthy of the name was made of."

Bottai, like a fox trapped in a corner, was on the attack. "You throw a daughter at me when I'm in my early seventies. Does that seem like a decent thing to do? In any case, I'll say it again: it still needs to be proven."

"A strand of hair'll do it."

"What do you mean?"

"Nowadays, you can pull a hair out and in five minutes the doctors will tell you where you come from. You should know that."

"Imagine if that information ended up in the wrong hands. I didn't wreck two families back then, I'm not about to do it now. Anyway, congratulations. You've had your revenge. You've found a way to make me drink myself to death good and proper. Are you happy now?"

"Everyone has their own Rosa."

"Shove it up your fucking ass, you and her."

"What on earth are you saying?"

"You burst into my life one evening, just like that, and you start stripping the paintwork off everywhere. Your life went wrong somewhere, and now you're ruining other people's, at a most sensitive time, what's more, when we're all getting ready to pull our oars in. I can picture you, you know, in that house up on the hill, with nothing but hogs around you, mulling over things, curdling your blood over how our affair could have gone differently . . . Do you know what I think? If history goes one way and not another it means it was meant to go that way. Period. Put your mind at rest."

"Well, there's a letter."

"What are you saying now?"

"You heard me perfectly well. A nice letter where I've written every single detail about our little romance. When it's time, it'll go where it needs to go."

Loriano felt the right side of his body collapse, and he regained his balance just in time. He was like an empty sack, waiting to be beaten. "What are you talking about?"

"Have all the glasses you've ever drunk gone to your brain at once? I said what I said."

"Where is it?"

"What?"

"The letter you're blathering on about."

"It's where it should be."

"What do you want to do with it?"

"Nothing. For your information, it's in the same envelope as my will. When the time comes, it'll be revealed to the person it is intended for."

"Laura."

"I owe it to her."

"Are you crazy? Not only her mother's death, but a slap in the face as well. Is that what you want?"

"It's better than knowing she'll have to live without finding out who she really is."

"It's pure egotism."

"That doesn't sound good coming from you."

"Laura has done nothing to deserve this. But since you've lost your head, you want to leave her a legacy like that so that you can cleanse your conscience and have the last word. There's nothing to cleanse, you know? Things went as they went. Telling her the truth will only send her to the madhouse. Don't you see?"

"Ah, now you're taking an interest in her."

"Of course, I'm interested in her. I'm not an animal."

"Spoke the wolf."

"Think about it. How would you take it, in her place?"

"Badly."

"Precisely. Exacting your revenge gives you more pleasure than leaving your daughter in peace."

"I know where you're going with this."

"Where am I going?"

"You're scared of a daughter you've never recognized as your own coming into the house and creating a scene."

"Are you stupid, or what? I never recognized her,

because I've only just found out now there's someone I need to recognize."

"Careful with your words."

Bottai understood one thing only: the only way to rein the madwoman in was to try to reason with her. He was surprised to find himself having a terrible thought. He imagined himself going over to Poggio Corbello in the middle of the night, stabbing Nives to death, and burning the whole place down, including the hen. Now, more than ever, hanging up on her was out of the question. He needed to keep the widow on the line. He forced himself to stay calm, but it wasn't easy. Inside, he was steaming over, on full throttle. "Listen, I'm sorry about everything. I'd like you to know that if I made any mistakes, I made them in good faith."

"You can't gut someone in good faith."

"Well then, I'll say this. I didn't have the courage. Am I supposed to kill myself for that?"

"Don't worry, the drink is doing that."

"Are you sure you have nothing to do with it?"

"With what?"

"The fact that I'm hammering myself to death, glass by glass."

"What?"

"I started back then."

"Not counting whatever run-up. I was there, and I saw you with my own eyes. The legend of you and Ferrari going through a 20-liter demijohn of wine in two days was circulating long before we were together."

"It got worse after that."

"You bought three apartments in Silvestri with your earnings. Anteo got everything wrong. With people as

spruced up as you around, he should have opened a gro-
cery store. He could have taken me to the sea every summer. At least that."

"You never left."

"That's what I'm telling you."

"Left my thoughts, I mean. I shouldn't be saying this,
since you like being the one in control, but the truth is this:
it was like an endless blitz."

"Now you're talking in riddles."

"Let me give you an idea of what it's like: I open my eyes
and that's what I think about; I close my eyes and that's
what I think about. The whole day is a torment. Then
someone tells you off if you drown yourself in drink to give
yourself courage . . . I understand. Looking at the game
board from your point of view, you were left alone by the
side of the road with a suitcase. If the tables were turned,
though, you wouldn't find paradise, I can assure you."

This sudden spurt of sentiment annoyed Nives. She held
the receiver away from her ear, as if she were listening to
the old vet's words through the grate of a wood-burning
stove. Loriano could feel the hesitation at the other end of
the line. He ploughed on. "You weren't the only one left at
the curve in the road outside Poggio Corbello. A certain
Bottai is still stuck there, on that October night. The liquor
I'd downed at the fall fair served the same purpose as ever:
to give me courage. I had to pull the plug on a situation that
was tying me down. I felt that, as with everything, the most
important thing was the first step. Once I'd taken that step,
everything else would work out on its own. I'd even
rehearsed it."

"How?"

"I made the most of the fact that Donatella was working

at the hairdresser's that afternoon, doing a few perms. I went home early, giving myself a clear hour of peace and quiet. I took out the sheet of paper where I'd written down everything that I needed to up-anchor and set sail at full speed to the other side of the world towards a new life with you. My best clothes, the two or three family heirlooms I was attached to . . . I placed the big suitcase on the bed. I'd become quite good at it by then: all the shelves, drawers, and cupboards, open and shut in record time. I knew how to pack everything into the suitcase, occupying every single inch. It gave me goosebumps to think that, if you wanted, you could erase your presence in your house in nine minutes."

"You take that long because you're a man. We women can do it in the blink of an eye."

"As proof of all my good intentions, there was the cash withdrawal from the bank. That clerk, Crocetta, helped me, even though it was nearly closing time. When I told him that I wanted to take ten million lire out of my account, he said, 'Hey, you'll leave us in our underwear!' Then, as a joke, he added, 'Are you off to the moon?' I didn't answer. My heart was beating like a drum. He saw I was in no mood for a chat and went to the safe. A minute later, he slapped the bills on the table. 'Shall I put them in a bag?' he asked, and I felt as though I were buying vegetables. Imagine how upset I was when I heard my name being called as soon as I set foot outside. It was Donatella, who'd finished early at the hairdresser's and had taken the opportunity to do a little shopping before heading home. I felt myself crumble to pieces. I told her I'd gone to the bank to sign a few papers. She swallowed the lie whole, only half listening; she's never paid any attention to our finances.

She didn't even glance at the little white brick I had tucked under my arm. Crocetta came out to lock up and saw my wife. 'Good day to you!' he said. 'Good day to you, Salvatore.' He noticed my fierce expression. Then he looked at the life's savings I was clutching to my chest. Who knows what went through his mind? In the end, he cleared his throat and left. I just stood there, a thousand pins pricking my face."

It was odd for Nives, after all those years, to picture these scenes from the other side. Bottai continued, "The idea of getting drunk was a stupid weakness, but I only realized it after I'd gotten into bed, with Donatella already sounding her bugle. I lay there as still as a mummy, and the trap was set: my eyelids started to droop. There were times when I woke up from a two-second snooze with a start, my heart in my throat. Had I missed the appointment? The minutes on my alarm clock went by as slow as a snail, or as fast as a hare. Until the time came. I climbed out of bed and went through the motions I'd practiced so many times. You should have seen me; I looked like a ballet dancer. I'd packed and unpacked my suitcase so many times that I was on automatic pilot. I soon realized I'd been an idiot, though. I hadn't taken the light through the windows into account. I could have closed the shutters or pulled the curtains. I made a failed attempt and bumped into door knobs and sharp corners. Nevertheless, my touch was that of an artist. They could have called me fairy fingers. I unzipped zippers and unbuckled buckles; I folded my clothes blindly, with Donatella there under the bedcovers. I told myself the missed period she'd told me about would come sooner or later; she'd never been late before. 'It's a curse of the devil, trying to lead me astray.'

That's what I thought as I moved around the room like a ghost. Finally, I carried the giant suitcase down to the front door. I was dripping with sweat. But I had to keep going, without rolling down the ravine that was haunting me: that is, my guilty conscience at leaving a wife behind, like a gutted cow, to be the laughing-stock of the town. At the door, like you, I remembered my ring. I was planning to grab the keys of the Fiat 127 from the plate we kept on the table and leave my ring there. But it wouldn't come off. My finger suddenly felt like the branch of an ash tree. I tugged and tugged at it. The effort made blood rush to my face. 'I'll cut it off!' All this while I was fighting not to listen to the other side, speaking loud and clear. 'You're not going anywhere,' the ring said. 'If you're so thirsty to see the world, take me with you. That or nothing.' I yanked even harder, jerking like a madman. When Donatella turned the light on in the hallway, she found me by the front door, my hair disheveled, heaving like a bull, looking as though I was beating myself up."

"Oh mother."

"I don't know what she saw. She was drowsy with sleep. 'You've gotten dressed,' she said, rubbing her eyes. I had my rain jacket on. Worse, the suitcase was two feet away. 'I was going to get a breath of air,' I said. I used to do it quite often, especially after a bad bout of drinking—one of those times when you don't pass out completely, but you lie in bed as if you are riding waves, the whole room transformed into a malicious carnival ride. Fernet has that effect on me, for example. Sometimes I woke up in the car, feeling as though I'd landed on another planet. 'Maybe the lasagna we had for dinner was a bit off,' Donatella said. Only then did I notice that she was deadly pale, a hand cradling her stomach. 'I feel like a brick is sitting right here.' A moment later her eyes opened wide, and she ran into the bathroom. What else could I do? I followed her. She'd even lost a little on her crazy run to the bathroom. I found her with her head down the toilet. A sign that her late period couldn't be ignored. In any case, I'd been found out."

"In the meantime, someone was dying of cold out on the curve of the road."

"It went on all night. Instead of taking on the world in my Fiat 127, I was washing vomit off the tiles. I couldn't stop thinking about you, whatever you say. A picture of you in mind, on the side of the road, waiting. By the time Donatella had gotten back to sleep, it was past two in the morning. I found myself nailed to the mattress, whereas, in another scenario, we had long passed Livorno already. I woke up still fully dressed and leaped to my feet immediately. My wife had already gotten up. I heard the usual bustling noises coming from the kitchen. She was already dressed. "What a night!" she said. She looked better, but she did everything to avoid my gaze: there was a cup to wash, barley coffee to serve, and so on. Finally, she realized she was late for work and deigned to look at me. 'Will I see you here for lunch?' She always asked me that, because if I had to treat animals in some of the farms in the area, I often preferred having a quick sandwich out. That day, however, her question was like an elephant smashing into the living room. I nodded, and she left. Even the way she slammed the door sounded different from usual. That was when I saw it. The suitcase was still there. Exhausted by everything that had happened in the night, I'd fallen asleep without putting my things away."

They both hung from those last words. Especially Nives, who suddenly felt as if they had cemented her mouth. Loriano was the first to break the silence. "Crocetta saw me come back with the same bundle of notes he'd given me the day before. This time, he didn't say a word. He put the money back into the safe, charged me the commission, and so long."

Reliving these events had emptied both of them out; the late hour was also beginning to take its toll. On one end, there was Loriano, who had received a pummeling and gone over so many episodes from his past that he felt full of holes; on the other end, there was Nives, who had suddenly been robbed of the rage that had been feeding her for half a lifetime, like a hearth hiding embers beneath the ashes. She felt a certain tenderness for Loriano now. In fact, she was surprised when those feelings she'd buried long ago broke over her like a wave. It's odd how an old flame can be rekindled at a certain age. She cleared her throat. In a tone that could have been that of a scared deer, she said, "Why didn't we seek one another out later, then?"

Bottai looked at himself in the mirror. Which, if it had been required to reflect the vet's sentiments entirely, would have shattered to pieces. "I don't know . . . I was ashamed, I suppose."

"I was really angry, you know."

"You vanished from the face of the earth; that much I remember."

"An avalanche like that would have buried anyone. Weeks went by before I found the courage to go back into town. I made up a thousand excuses not to go to Thursday market."

"Not like anyone would have shot you."

"If that had been the problem, I would have camped in the middle of Piazza San Bastiano. I would have gone in front of a firing squad. But just the idea of seeing you again made me feel like I was dying. When it finally happened, you'd bought yourself a flashy car."

"Two idiots."

"Speak for yourself."

"I was lost in a vale of shame. You were as angry as the devil himself."

"Worse."

"And we lost one another."

"Worse."

"We threw each other away."

"Then Anteo told me one morning that he'd called you."

"Yes."

"There was that little donkey that suddenly started behaving as if it were possessed, rasping and foaming at the mouth, rolling on the ground. When he started kicking himself in the belly it was too much. It was heart-wrenching to watch. Sheriff. That's what he was called. Because he used to defend us from trespassers. Every time someone he didn't know came along, he'd start braying with his front hooves up on the fence. He did Roy's job. Our lovely Alsatian would wag his tail happily at anyone, even snakes. Bless him."

"I can see him now, that donkey. He was a trouble-maker, alright. He was suffering from colic. I would get cramps just thinking about being called out to Poggio Corbello for those emergencies."

"I stayed in the house the whole time. In fact, as soon

as I heard the engine on the big road, I locked myself in my room. I sat there, knowing a certain Bottai was just a few yards away. Not knowing which way to turn, I took to praying. What an idiot I was."

"I nearly lost an eye trying to take care of that big baby. All of a sudden, I got a horseshoe in the face. I still have the scar. It'd never happened before and it never happened again. I can usually feel the animals, you know. Just to give you an idea where my head was that day. From one moment to the next, that ass kicked me back to reality."

"I could have strangled you! I heard you calling me from outside. 'Nives! Nives!' I wanted to die. By the time I got there, you were already in a pool of blood."

"I didn't know what had happened. I walked around without knowing what I was doing. It was far worse than a hangover . . . Poor old Anteo was guiding me, and all the while there was the voice of a little Loriano inside me saying, 'Don't you dare say anything you'll regret!' I had no idea whether my ravings were audible on the outside. The next thing I knew, I was sitting in an armchair."

"Two towels."

"What?"

"Two towels drenched in blood."

"What was I saying?"

"Nothing. You were looking around, your eyes like an owl's. Meanwhile, my poor husband was going out of his mind; he was already planning to get his rifle out and shoot the poor animal. He was worried about being sued or something. He was also worried we could get rabies."

"There was one moment that only I could have known about."

"Which was?"

"In the middle of that colossal discombobulation—not even the slap Maciste gave me when I was twenty had the same effect, though I walked around for a week with no feeling on the right side of my face and a buzz in my ear that lasted a month or two—all of a sudden the chaos calmed, the curtain parted, and I saw you."

"A right sight."

"You had your hair tied up high, but two curls had freed themselves and had fallen over your face."

"I bet. I was wringing out cloths nineteen to the dozen. You had a gash across your forehead that wouldn't stop bleeding."

"Everything was blurry, except your face. Anteo's words sounded as though they were rising out of a well a hundred miles deep."

"Getting kicked in the head by a donkey will do that."

"That's what you do to me."

"Come off it. Then the ambulance came."

"I can't even remember."

"When they took you away, I nearly fainted. I ended up in the armchair you'd been sitting in two minutes before. Now there's a hen who's taken a turn sitting there, embalmed with Tide."

"I came back to my senses the next day with two memories: a massive headache, and a picture of you, with two rebellious curls. They told me not to go to sleep, but that was all I wanted to do, so that I could dream of you on top of me. Donatella gave me a shake every time I stared into space. Tears dripped down my face for no reason."

"They said it was the head trauma."

"I spent a month like that, checking everything I did. It's not that I wasn't able to move; the doctor ordered me

not to. Even when I turned my neck, I had to take pre-
cautions. I wanted to wing it over to Poggio Corbello in a
second and say to you, 'Quietly now. Let's leave.' With no
bags this time, no money, nothing. We would have rein-
vented our lives in Palma de Mallorca, or in the desert surrounded by camels. I didn't care a hoot about America.
America was you."

Nives caught her breath. For a second, she stepped out
of her skin and saw a film sequence: she and Loriano, who
knows where; a whole life of what could have been but had
never happened spinning by. A poisoned candy that she
reluctantly put aside. Her hands itched. How stupid she'd
been to give up so easily! It was true that the vet hadn't
exactly played easy to get . . . One October evening, after
all that wild partying at the fall festival, the fate of two
lovers had been sealed by an upset stomach. If only
Donatella hadn't been so greedy that night . . . all of a sudden, she felt sorry for her. To stay in a marriage even while
knowing that one night her husband had been on the
verge of letting her bleed out, abandoned. The ugliest kind
of abandonment, with no explanation, like a thief. By con-
trast, Nives had kept her side of the bargain. Okay, her
escape had fizzled out thirty yards from her front door, but
that hadn't been her fault. As far as she was concerned, she
had one point over him in that department. The widow
felt a wave of heat flow through her: in the light of the latest confessions, she was better able to understand the
obstacles that had been put in the way of their elopement.
She felt like a kid who'd just tripped over on the gravel
and had to get herself up, with grit in her palms and grazes
on her backside, without even a friend to beat up as pay-
back. Nives realized she was doing something unheard of:

she was forgiving him. It came naturally to her. She could see why: it was a new prison that she hadn't gotten used to yet. In some ways it pacified her; at the same time, it ripped her to pieces. Without anger, she was nothing. "Maybe you were right," she said, her voice sticking in her throat. "It would have been better not to talk about it."

This felt like the right moment for Bottai to make his surprise attack. "What do you need the letter for, then?"

Nives had to make a karate move with her thoughts. She'd been on such a different wavelength that for a second she had no idea what Loriano was talking about. It was like being shaken out of a daydream. She didn't like the situation she found herself in once she was back on earth one bit. She was on her own in the house at Poggio Corbello, her soul torn apart, and her legs aching from standing up and talking on the phone for so long. Nonetheless, one nerve in particular had been prodded, and she answered on an impulse, "Tell me, is that all you can think about?"

Loriano bit his lip, cursing under his breath. He had prepared a juicy dish, and now he'd spilled it just as it was doing its magic. He tried to reclaim a little ground by saying, "It still seems offensive to me, considering what we once were."

Nives was already sharpening her fingernails, her eyes bulging like a devil's. "Are you wooing me with memories? Do I look stupid to you?"

"What are you saying?"

"Don't pretend not to understand."

"If something happened, I didn't notice."

"Bravo! All that talk about lasagna and vomit, bank withdrawals, hallucinations after a donkey kick, and so on.

I'd almost fallen for it. How can you look at yourself in the mirror?"

That was exactly what Bottai was doing at that moment. He looked away quickly. "Did I say anything wrong?"

Just like that, she was the old Nives again, if not worse: rivers of resentment. She gripped the receiver as if it were a sword and barked down the phone. "You great big ugly snail! You pirate! You ball-breaking namby-pamby! You're the worst kind of traitor!" A word came to her that seemed to sum up all her woes; she fired it up, forming a ball of flames to shoot from the mouth of a volcano, "Bastard!"

The word reached Loriano like a firebomb which knocked his head off. He realized he was lost. "But Nives . . ." he spluttered.

She was in the throes of an epic moment: she was crying. She hadn't done so even at Anteo's funeral. But now she was. Because, Holy God, she couldn't go on any longer. With all those reminiscences he'd played her with, she felt abandoned once again at the side of the road. Bottai had really been an evil sorcerer. First, he'd taken her on a flight to paradise lost, encouraging her to open up her heart, which she'd protected for centuries. Then he'd stuck the knife in for his own self-serving reasons. That is, the matter of the letter. He was trying to make sure it didn't get around too much. It was the worst slap in the face he could have meted out to her. Big fat tears dropped down her face in a waterfall. She'd been humiliated, especially by herself; she'd dug her grave with her own hands. Moreover, there was an undeniable fact: how could she hold it against Loriano, when all he wanted to do was protect what he'd built up over a lifetime? All that was left for her was solitude. Once her husband had died, she was left standing there in her slippers, naked, like the old women in children's nursery rhymes, sleeping with a hen on her bedside table. She couldn't breathe through her sobs. Every shudder felt like it was turning her stomach upside-down. In the end, though, disarmed, she managed to say it, the receiver dangling under her chin, "Alright then, I'll throw it away."

Bottai was about to catch the ball on the rebound, but he felt a twinge somewhere inside. He saw himself as an executioner, and he didn't like playing that part. The widow was making him out to be a rascal, one of those men who selfishly play with people's feelings. In an imperious tone of voice, he said, "Let God strike me down if one word of what I've said isn't true!"

Nives was still weeping. Her tears continued to flow; she couldn't control them. She was gasping for breath. The taste of snot on her lips. She somehow managed to say, "It doesn't matter."

Loriano was in the right, but he refused to put on the costume required to finish the duel. It was true, he had dwelled on the past in order to soften her up a little. But being cast as a devil, who had harked back to an old love affair for his own convenience, was too much. There was no way he was going to sacrifice the sentiments of the past. "You've gotten the wrong end of the stick, as usual."

"At least you had a little fun."

Bottai was offended, despite himself. "Nives, come back to earth now."

"I've been back on earth since '82."

"All I'm saying is that it would be crazy to drag other people down just to dot your i's and cross your t's."

"So, I've been alive all this time just to say yes to every-thing, to let events roll over me like a bulldozer while I stay as quiet as a mouse?"

"All you need is a little common sense."

"I get dumped, I bring up a daughter with a father on loan, and now, on top of everything, I get an earful from you."

"I don't need to convince you of anything. If you prefer to drop a bomb with your letter, feel free. I'm just telling you that there's no need; your plan to settle scores would break many other people's hearts. You wouldn't even be there to watch the show."

By that point, Nives was playing with an open hand. She didn't even hear what she was saying as she said it: "And yet, it's the only way I can leave a mark." She only realized afterwards that she'd laid herself completely bare: her death would cause an earthquake in several families. The only card she had left would burn down what little she'd built.

"Do you really like the idea of being cursed by your daughter?"

The widow trembled. "Why should she?"

"I would, if I were her. My mother dies and at the lawyer's office throws a hand-grenade from the grave. Nice gift, eh? To obtain what? The boundary between truth and punishment is very fine indeed."

"Now you've become a philosopher."

"Even a child would understand."

"There you are; I'm an idiot now."

"Certain things are best left as they are."

"One day, Banda will come with my usual two bags of shopping, he'll knock at the door, and there'll be no answer. He'll have a shock and call the fire station. The fields and the property will be sold to whoever offers the most, and that's it, *arrivederci*, everything is erased. My only daughter will have no reason to set foot in this shit-hole. The only gossip that will fly around will be that, after her husband's death, Nives went a little soft in the head and even started talking to her hens . . . But I was here, for God's sake! I had a little happiness in my lifetime. I want people to know!"

"Nobody's saying you didn't."

"Everybody else has had a romance they can talk about, or that people still gossip about years later. I haven't. The only affair I'd like to shout out to the world is a fire cracker that would set at least two houses on fire, if not three. It's a nice story, with a sad ending. It's about a lover abandoned on the side of the road at midnight."

"You sound as if the rest of your life has been worth-less—"

"Don't put any other words in my mouth."

"Is that what I was doing?"

"I didn't give a damn the day Laura was born."

Nives could lob cannonballs like that with no warning. Loriano instinctively took a step back, batting his eyelids repeatedly. "I may not have gotten what you just said."

"I've never said it out loud."

He cleared his throat. "Some advice: don't do it again. It's a blasphemous thing to say."

"And yet, it's true. Even today I pity her, poor thing. Not only did she have a father who wasn't her father, she also had a mother who had fallen out of love with her when she was still in her belly. That must be why she was born two months early. She could feel things were not right, so she got moving."

Loriano didn't know what to say. His arms were full of goosebumps. He saw himself in the past; his first thought was, 'Whose arms was I about to throw myself into?' Then he put things back into focus. On the other end of the line was a person who'd been hurt. In the meantime, Nives went on; a new channel for her grievances had been opened up. "To begin with, there was no problem. In fact, finding out I was pregnant felt like a seal of love that would lead in a certain direction. There was nothing on paper yet, but the idea that Anteo might somehow have been involved didn't even cross my mind: he always came back from the fields a wreck; he could hardly stop himself nodding off during supper. Three or four glasses of wine did the rest. For the love of God, once in a blue moon he'd consecrate our marriage. But he would always be half-asleep, all limp, his eyeballs rolling back into his head. All the while, a Fiat 127 the color of diarrhea would park near the cane thicket practically every day at a certain time. We used to keep an eye on my husband, as clouds of dust were thrown up against the horizon by his tractor. The little car creaked. After our acrobatics, we would promise each other the world, our hearts in our mouths. Dripping with sweat and as beautiful as a summer's day. You may have an image of me printed on your retina after the donkey kick, but I have one of you, too: a bronze god, in the rear-view mirror of that tin can. I didn't need a scientist to help me weigh the relative probabilities of one or the other of you having doused me."

Put this way, Bottai felt sick to the stomach. Nonetheless, a memory came back to him in a flash: one day in particular that summer, when he'd been as thin as an anchovy with all that humping in the triple heat of the car. He could almost smell it. He could see her pale white breasts. Just as she did back then, Nives rode on. "One morning, I caught Anteo and ruined his barley coffee. 'Listen,' I said. 'There's been nothing for three months.' He was dipping a cookie; I can see him right here as if it were yesterday. He sat there, the cookie suspended mid-air between the cup and his mouth for a while, as if he were exploring the consequences of my words and knowing full well where the confines of his responsibility lay. His comment was succinct. If I were to think of the precise moment when the earth shifted under the feet of several people, it would be that one. He muttered, "At least we know how much to ask Bandini." He was already thinking of renting out the fields he couldn't manage; Anteo wasn't the type to hire work-hands. It's funny to think that the rent money goes straight to the Languedoc, to a country I've never seen and never want to see."

Bottai's eyelids were beginning to sag. He was in bad shape from all that reliving of the past; he tried to move the conversation forward. "In any case . . ."

The vet's attempts to stall her were ignored completely. Nives was steaming ahead on her own train of thought and had every intention of getting to the end of it, however many cars were hooked onto the locomotive. "After being abandoned by the side of the road, I started to feel the weight of being pregnant, in every sense. It no longer felt like a blessing; that glob of anxiety came to life. It grew week after week, and I couldn't do anything about it. Everything exasperated me, even poor Anteo's devotion; he'd gone the other way, sticking to me like a tick, crazy about me. Months went by with Laura macerating in my womb, that sea of woe. She ate what I ate, and in addition she had to absorb the stinkweed of my days. I carried on to the bitter end, on my hands and knees. After you bought that fancy car and had your face kicked in by the donkey, things got even worse. I felt as though I was nursing the biggest turd of the century. My only comfort was that it was a girl; if it had been a boy, I think I would have hanged myself from the apricot tree. I really couldn't bear the idea of bringing up a miniature vet whose damned buccaneering spirit might blossom one day. A little girl would be better camouflaged. Anyway, it meant being satisfied with very little. The message I read was this: I'd been repudiated, with the bonus of a baby to bring up, who would remind me every single day of the foolishness I'd imagined I could undertake. In the midst of that seaquake, news of the happy event in the Bottai household reached my ears. The first thing I thought was to kill myself for real, take a pair of scissors to my belly. The situation was clear, after all: you'd used me to unload yourself, then you went back home and unloaded again with your wife. In the end, I was the injured party. Adding insult to injury, as the saying goes. Worse than injury: slaughter."

Loriano felt it was his duty to strike a blow. "Nives, I explained in detail how—" Again, the widow sidestepped him, like a bullet traveling a thousand miles an hour whizzing past his ear. "I gave birth to her on the first of May. Anteo stuck a pink rosette up on the door. It felt like a funeral wreath in my memory. I stared at Laura a lot, but I hardly ever touched her. I was looking for details that would make my hair stand on end: the shape of her hands, or her nose. I had to swallow the nausea that I felt when I latched her to my teat. She was a voracious little frog; she suckled like the devil, until my nipples bled. And the emotion that dictated my life surfaced: my milk had dried up, but she still demanded tons of it. I started feeding her formula. When we went into town on Sundays, we bumped into you, the happy family . . . you'd perfected your disappearing act whenever you smelled our presence in the air."

"I thought the same about you."

"Meaning?"

"You were just as ready to give it out in the cane thicket as you were in your bedroom."

"Take that back, now!"

"That's what it looked like from my side of things."

"You were using a yardstick that had nothing to do with me."

"The night after our appointment on the road, you show up pregnant. That fact answered all my questions. Of course, I disappeared: the idea of meeting your eyes was enough to send me straight to the bottle. I'd been at it, by the way, the day Anteo called me to tend to that devil of a donkey."

"We got used to it over time."

"Time does that: it sends everything down."

"At the nursery school gate, we would say good morning to one another like acquaintances who never take the plunge and actually become friends."

"It was the same at the door of the elementary school."

"I used to put on my makeup with palpitations. 'Please let him not be there,' I begged to myself. 'Let him not be there.'"

"Whenever Donatella had a cold, I wanted to shrivel up and die: it became my job to take Amedeo to school and pick him up at the last bell. When I saw you coming, I felt as though my hair was being pulled out, but I pretended nothing was going on."

"Homework, school trips. I spied on you through these events. I heard Laura's stories about the class—"

"Me too. Birthday parties were a test of our character. By the evening I was panting for a drink."

"Those interminable summers . . . then the kids grew up."

"After middle school, they went about on their own."

"Then there was high school."

"That was hard."

"School itself was not the problem, Loriano."

"True."

"When Laura came home with the news, I had to sit myself down."

"It was a shock for me, too. That was probably when my hair started dropping out."

"Brother and sister!"

"I couldn't have known that. But I thought of all the rest, and it made me feel ill."

"Brother and sister, going on eighteen, start looking at one another in that way. Amedeo would drive here to pick her up, and I stopped eating. I lost pounds and pounds. My poor husband kept saying, 'Come on, it's not such a big deal. She'll have to go out into the world at some point . . . I imagined them in the cane thicket, just like us twenty-odd years before. I felt like retching all the time. But there's more: what if a squirt got in by mistake? Everybody knows that close relatives shouldn't get into each other's pants; mutants are born. I couldn't do anything. Say anything. I was all skin and bones, I was up all night. Amedeo even gave her a little ring, and I asked the doctor to prescribe me some strong drops. Laura was looking gorgeous . . . Listen, talking about it gives me shivers, even now."

"Maybe part of their attraction was because of that fact, their common blood—"

"Of course it was. They were knocked sideways by their abnormal love; Laura never wanted to leave his side. Then there were the phone calls . . . the bills that came were like a slap in the face. I had to put up with having her little boyfriend in the living room. I couldn't stand listening to their lovey-dovey talk! The last thing I needed was for them to be in the bedroom, doing what they couldn't do outside, for lack of time or somewhere decent."

"At that age a board full of nails is enough."

"I certainly didn't encourage the affair. I had to put up with her hysterical outbursts; I'd suddenly become the wicked witch. If it'd been for me, I'd have kept her locked in a room, chained to the wall. One evening she started raving, talking about getting married. That was when I really lost it."

"Amedeo marched into the room like a soldier and said, 'I need to tell you something.' When he'd communicated his intention, Donatella reacted like a hyena. 'That's complete nonsense,' she shrieked. 'First, you need to focus on school.'"

"Good woman."

"But it wasn't enough. Our son had made his mind up. He's always been stubborn. All I could think about was you on the bride's side of the aisle on their wedding day . . . From star-crossed lovers to co-parents-in-law. I said to myself, 'What kind of curse is this?' And yet, I could see there was something poetic there, some essence of life: they were carrying on our work; they were completing what we didn't have the courage to do."

"What poetry? It wasn't poetry! It was incest between half-brother and sister; that's what it was!"

"I didn't know that. You could have confided in me."

"And risk starting the third world war?"

"Luckily it fizzled out in the end, as many love affairs at that age do. Amedeo wanted to kill himself."

"I'm the one you should thank for that."

"How come?"

"I couldn't allow them to sink into the quagmire we'd created without their knowing it. Between them, they could have given life to an abomination. Even aside from that, imagining them hand in hand was enough to make me shudder."

"So?"

"Putting a spoke in the wheel for two eighteen-year-olds is not that difficult."

"Nives, I can't believe it."

"You'd better believe it. I went to see a specialist."

"A specialist?"

"I paid with something that never goes out of currency."

"What?"

"The flesh of a young girl in bloom."

"Who?"

"Laura."

Loriano wondered whether he was ready for yet another turn of events. He could feel another bomb ready to go off. The answer was no; he wasn't ready. But he could no longer avoid it. "Did you use your daughter?"

"*Our* daughter."

"Well, her. Yes."

"She was a bouncy little rabbit, craving love."

"Careful. You're talking about the person you gave birth to."

"She was itching with desire, and other hormonal calamities. I knew someone who was unparalleled in navigating the territory."

"Who?"

"Look up at the ceiling."

"What?"

"If you look up at the ceiling, there's a clue."

Bottai did her bidding: he looked up. He saw there was mold in the corners of the plastered ceiling. That was when he got the hint. He said quickly, "Renato?"

"Who better than him?"

Loriano had to fight off dizziness, not for the first time. After three hours on the phone, there was Pagliuchi tumbling down on his head again. He asked himself whether the person on the other end of the line hadn't planned the whole thing from the beginning, laying a trail to a place they were now getting to. The idea crushed him. A simple, countryside vet like him was like a speck of dust compared to a mind as sophisticated as hers. Discouraged, he said, "My friend, what did you do this time?"

"We were talking about it earlier. Renato still chases twenty-year-olds today. He was more popular back in the day, but since when has the old seducer lost his touch?"

"So?"

"I asked him."

"What?"

"To play the lovesick Romeo."

"Wait, let me be clear here. You asked Renato Pagliuchi

to court a girl who had just turned eighteen?" A shiver of horror ran from his head to his toes as he said this.

"If I were to tell you about the flings the old sailor has had in every port, we'd be on the phone forever."

"I'm not interested."

"A pureblood that—"

"Nives, move on please."

"Laura was pining from morning till night for that young trickster who wasn't even old enough to have a beard."

"Hey, go easy. That's my boy you're talking about."

"A professional like Pagliuchi could brush away an ant like him just like that."

"You're making me angry now. Let me tell you, my Amedeo is—"

"Girls fell in love with Renato's good looks, for sure, but there was all his other magic, too. His gaze, for example. They'd drop into that well with no hesitation. His words, his touch. Try lying down on a bed with that old fox. He was a war dog who could strip the panties off the Virgin Mar—"

"Stop! I won't allow this!"

"Whatever. I could see the effect he would have on a young grasshopper with hardly any experience."

"That's disgusting."

"A man of experience, do you know what I mean?"

"Disgusting."

"He accepted without reservation."

"When I see him, I'll punch his face in."

"It took him a week."

"He'd better not knock on my door ever again!"

"I watched Laura. She'd come home with a hooded

look, but it wasn't sadness. She'd suddenly found herself up in the clouds, on her way to Mars. During dinner, she'd go off for minutes at a time, a cunning look on her face. The same we used to have when we were girls. Including Donatella."

"That's enough, please."

"I knew it was a terrible thing I was doing; I'm not evil."

"Please excuse me if I harbor some doubts."

"It was anyway better than her committing incest without knowing it. Another notable feature of Pagliuchi's is his hunger."

"So, you needed to feed him bread, too."

"No, no, he had plenty of that. Though he was as thin as a rake—"

"I really don't care."

"Hunger for women. It wasn't his fault, in the end; he was just made that way. He was a big shot with the amorous arts engraved in his body and soul."

"To my eyes, he's just a poor bastard obsessed with filling every hole he comes across because he can't satisfy his own. I'm going to have a chat with him one of these days."

"You stay there and philosophize away. Renato beds young girls without saying much at all. Which is what happened to Laura. She was so young, it only took him twenty minutes to woo her with his turbine engine. When she came out of it, she didn't even know what her name was."

"I'm going to be sick."

"Yes, it could have that effect. Being with Pagliuchi was worse than riding a roller-coaster: immense pleasure, but your knees were like jelly when you got off. Laura was like you in front of a glass of wine: she swore it would be the last time, and then, one minute later, she was begging for more and more. I could see it. Abstinence from Renato was hard on her. A mother knows these things."

"I'd better not say anything."

"Take a fresh flower like her and put her in the hands of someone like Amedeo, who's just woken up to the facts of life and can hardly find his dick to go and piss. Then give her one minute of ass-slapping from a bulldozer like Renato, and you'll see the mush that's left at the end. Guided by a hand that knows what it's doing, it only takes three sessions to turn a girl into a woman. Laura got the complete treatment. Suddenly, a sophisticated side blossomed in her."

"She became a slut, in other words."

"Now I'm going to come over and give you a handful."

"Let's get this clear: in this game, I have to accept my Amedeo being torn to bits, while your little butterfly can't be touched?"

"*Ours.*"

"Whatever. Get on with this pile of shit, will you?"

"You should have seen her. She was no longer herself. There were fewer and fewer phone calls, which Anteo appreciated. On Sunday afternoons, Laura would go into town by bus without waiting for her kissy-wissy boyfriend, who saw himself as a man, to pick her up in his crappy little car."

"Not that again."

"Laura was going other places. She'd come back in the evening with bags under her eyes. She'd start on her homework, completely placated. The agreement with Renato was clear: he was supposed to carry on until I was sure disaster had been averted. For him it was fine. He's always been so obliging . . ."

"I'm going to kill him."

"One evening, he was there at the front door."

"Who?"

"Amedeo. I answered. When I opened the door, there he was. With no warning. He was in a bad way. I've never seen anyone transformed that way by pain. He stammered something inaudible. The first thing I thought was that he'd faint on the steps. He was looking for Laura. He needed to speak to her at any cost. 'One moment,' I said. And left him there."

"You didn't even let him come in?"

"In this house, there was really no need for any more Bottais. I went to call our daughter; she was curved over, writing in her secret diary. She snapped it shut. We don't need to go into the scenes she was probably describing . . . When I told her there was a scared little boy at the door for her, she tossed her eyes. She let out a sigh that confirmed I would soon be singing victory."

"And then?"

"It took quite a while to shake off the little insect. We could hear him imploring, begging for an explanation, but his appeals were returned to the sender. Poor Anteo pitied the boy: he was racked, breaking into sobs that would end up in a fit of coughing. My poor husband said, 'Let's at least sit him down here at the table and talk things through calmly.' Over my dead body. In fact, I wanted Laura to annihilate him. So that in the Bottai household the cruel pangs of abandonment would finally be felt, the ones that drive you crazy, when heaven and earth no longer have any meaning and you yearn for only one thing: to leave this world. Living with pain like that is crazy."

"But he was just a boy."

"When Laura came back in, she made herself a cup of tea."

"Good for her."

"Then she went back to her room, and that was the last we heard of it. But I waited to talk to Renato. I let them carry on for another two long weeks. Getting rid of a cry-baby like that is not easy; Amedeo kept on leaving little messages and things like that. Ambushing her, fits of rage. It all played into my hand, as Laura was falling out of love with him fast. One day, she came home in tears. She'd been slapped."

"Impossible. My Amedeo would never—"

"He raised his hands to her, yes he did. Showing he was an idiot as well as a bore. The affair even turned Anteo against him; he was ready to come over to your place to set things straight, with a few kicks in the ass if necessary. 'I can't do it to the boy, but I can to his father,' he said, moving the furniture around the room to vent his anger. I'll tell you the truth, though: I liked the idea. I wouldn't have been sorry to see some trouble coming in your direction, as evidence of an old score to settle. In the end, I calmed him down. I couldn't lose sight of my objective, though I'd pretty much achieved it by then. Amedeo dug his own grave with that slap."

"Just so you know, Anteo wouldn't have done anything of the kind. He was intelligent enough to know how a boy who'd been rejected might behave."

"He split the wardrobe door in two with a punch. I had to give him the drops I was taking or he would have wrecked the whole house. Then there was you."

"If you'd seen the state my son was in, you'd be talking less. He locked himself in his room for days. He stopped eating; all he could do was cry."

"Good."

"Donatella was worried. She spent her days sitting in front of Amedeo's door. She was scared he'd do something stupid. No school. No friends. His life was over."

"I know what you mean."

"One day I put my foot down. We sent him to Siena to stay with my brother. A change of air would be good for him. Seeing new faces and all that. He finished high school there. Even now he hates coming back here."

"Same for Laura. I told Renato to stop his therapy; you can imagine the drama. Her grade-point average was down, but she managed to graduate. The first thing she said when she was done was, 'I want to leave.' A few days later we took her to Florence to look for accommodation; that's where she went to college."

Bottai sighed deeply. "Poor kids," he said.

"There was no other way. Or would you rather be spoon-feeding a deformed grandchild right now?"

"I don't know."

"In my letter, I apologize for that, too."

"What?"

"I tell Laura how Pagliuchi saved her from committing incest, about her father who isn't her father, and all the rest."

"Are you gone in the head?"

"She has the right to know. She may even understand what I, as a mother, had to do. I couldn't allow my idiocy to have consequences for her."

"Now, more than ever, you should throw that letter in the fire. You tell her the father she's still grieving for is a sham and that her real father is still alive. You tell her she made love to her own flesh and blood and that she was used by Pagliuchi, when he was on this way to forty, to avoid irreparable harm. All this in your last will and testament, that is, after the grievous event of your death. Nives, people lose their minds for much less. Even I, when I hang up, will never be the same again."

"Why is it that everything concerning me has to stay in the shadows?"

"It's common sense. We shouldn't talk about our joyriding all that time ago; it'll ruin our children's lives. For what? To prove that you've had some adventures? It wouldn't even be revenge against me."

"Even Rosaltea left the stage in a way that will be remembered. People still talk about it."

"Now you're harping on about that poor girl again. Come on, let her rest in peace."

"Anyway, nobody is going to convince me that Bardo didn't have something to do with that tragedy."

"Nives, not everyone's life has a false bottom hiding the truth, you know. Rosa was madly in love with Renato. She couldn't imagine life without him; she hated watching him do the rounds between wives, widows, sisters, and nieces instead of being with her. In the end, she did something stupid. By the way—"

"What?"

"According to the terrible story you've told me, Pagliuchi must know all about us."

"He doesn't know a thing."

"You tricked him into courting Laura without an excuse? I don't believe you."

"It was enough for him that my daughter had gone soft in the head with love and was putting her education and, more generally, her whole existence in jeopardy with all that humbug about marriage. The boyfriend needed to vanish."

"And he didn't bat an eye? Didn't he think it was crazy?"

"There were reasons enough."

"To explain why a mother would be trying to sell him her daughter's precious jewels? There are usually other ways to set a son or daughter straight when they have been waylaid by a crush. You gave him your girl's fresh untouched panties to play with."

"You don't know him."

"We grew up together."

"I mean his wolfish expression when he smells fresh meat. Renato has this weakness: if you talk to him about a woman that he hasn't yet had his way with, he won't stop until he gets her."

"Good quality, that."

"He lives for it. You have your wine; he likes branding young heifers."

"Only to grow old and die alone."

"That's the way his Rosa works."

"What about yours? Since you're so great at reciting other people's curses. What is your Rosa?"

"Solitude."

Her answer touched him. In the light of all her revelations, the vet understood how his old flame might feel abandoned. "Every one of us has that," he said, trying to lighten the load for her.

"Today it has manifested itself in its purest essence: the hen."

"Ah yes, the hen." Loriano's head spun; he felt as though he'd just returned from a long journey. Since the beginning of the phone call, he'd raced through a mass of details from his past: from Donatella's adolescent intrigues to the mystery of Rosaltea; from Pagliuchi's portraits as Jesus Christ to the artist's murder; from the cane thicket to the matter of the missed appointment at the road; from the realization he had a daughter to everything else. Now Nives was rewinding the tape and starting from the beginning: the embalmed hen. Her U-turn had been so abrupt that he could almost feel his blood running the wrong way. It felt like a good moment to move the conversation on and change tone. "How is she?"

The widow turned around to check. The receiver fell out of her hand. Loriano sensed that a cataclysm had occurred on the other end of the line. Finally, Nives picked up the phone again. "Listen," she said, "She's not there."

"Not there?"

"Giacomina, I mean."

"Where is she?"

"How am I supposed to know? She was sitting there, mummified. Now she's not there."

"So, she woke up."

"That's what it looks like. But I can't find her."

"Maybe she went to look for some chicken feed?"

"Dear God, she scares me."

"Who?"

"Giacomina."

"You said you were sleeping together."

"Knowing she's wandering around the house like a ghost makes me shit my pants."

"Nives, don't talk nonsense."

"Easy for you to say. You have a bugler in your room to keep you company with her snoring."

Loriano lurched back to reality again; picturing Donatella through all their stories, he'd almost forgotten she was in the house. "Wait," he whispered. He listened out for her. After a second, he said, "I can't hear a thing."

"Why are you talking like a spy?"

"Quiet!" hissed the vet.

"Who?"

"Donatella."

"What about her?"

"She's not snoring."

"She must have turned on her side. She's built like a ship, so the roaring from her stern is probably drowned in her breasts."

"You don't know her."

"We grew up together."

"I've slept in the same bed with her for a lifetime."

"That's news! Wait, let me write it down."

"I'm saying it's not a normal silence."

"Silence is silence."

"Maybe she's awake."

"Don't be so stupid; it's nearly two in the morning."

"And if she is awake?"

"Let's concentrate on my little hen who's gotten it in her head to be a ghost."

"I'll come over to Poggio Corbello right now and wring your neck and hers."

"Nice way to say thank you."

"You're turning my life upside-down, and I'm supposed to thank you for it?"

"Why are you mistreating me now?"

"I'm mistreating you?"

"To tell the truth, you've never stopped."

"Nives, there's a second phone in our bedroom."

"Am I supposed to care?"

"What if Donatella woke up because she realized I wasn't in bed? What if she picked up the phone, realizing I was still in the hall?"

"Donatella, are you there?"

"What?"

"Donatella, are you listening?"

"Stop it, you idiot."

"I'm here."

". . ."

". . ."

"Carry on, the two of you. This nocturnal melodrama is fun."

". . ."

"D-d-darling, I didn't . . ."

"Ciao, Donatella."

"Ciao, Nives. News of your hen?"

"I don't know. It gives me goosebumps. The idea that someone is wandering around my house without my knowing it makes me shudder."

"I know."

"Honey, I'll put the phone down and—"

"Dear, will you come and show me?"

"What?"

"How good you are at clearing out of the house in nine minutes."

"No, you don't understand . . . I was joking. Ha! You fell for it!"

"Shoes and all."

"You don't really believe that—"

"Nives, I'm really sorry."

"Dear friend, don't take it badly. What's happened has happened."

"Thanks for Amedeo, too."

"Mother's duty."

"As for Rosa, I agree with you. Bardo will take his sins to hell. In the meantime, he's sitting in an old people's home with senile dementia and can't recognize anyone or anything. While we're on the theme of revenge, Renato talks to me about it sometimes. He says he's never been a great fan of prayer, but for the last ten years or so, he's been lighting a candle for the Virgin Mary every week. He's praying that his father will live as long as possible. He goes to the home and congratulates the nurses for keeping his body going so perfectly. But the man's mind is another matter: he has fleeting moments of clarity, which make things more painful for him. Then he forgets everything all over again and most of the time doesn't even know his own name. He despairs, he cries . . . that's the price he's paying for the beatings he gave his son when he was a boy. And for having exploited a young girl when she already had enough problems of her own."

"It serves him right."

"Can I say something now?"

"Dear hubby, haven't you vented enough already?"

"Darling, let me put the phone down now, and we'll talk about this properly."

"Stop calling me 'darling'!"

"Donatella, for God's sake!"

"Ah, so now you're getting angry, are you? You're almost behaving like a man."

"None of it is true."

"None of what?"

"You know, come on."

"I don't. Not at all."

"Let's hang up. Then we can talk eye to eye."

"I think it's a good idea for Nives to hear what you have to say."

"Have you all gone crazy this evening?"

"Nives, are you crazy?"

"I've never been saner."

"You see? Come on dear, what do you have to say?"

"About the suitcase. That cursed October."

"Yes."

"I didn't rehearse packing so that I could elope with this crazy woman."

"But I still remember that sleepless night. I haven't touched lasagna since."

"Your stomach upset was the writing on the wall for me."

"So, it's true. You were thinking of eloping."

"I don't know. We did promise each other we would . . . As a matter of fact, she was the one who insisted. I only said 'yes' because I wanted to get down to business with her in that stinky cane thicket."

"Bastard!"

"Nives, don't you start, too. We were kids. In any case, the proof is that there was no suitcase at the end of the corridor. Donatella, tell me that's not the truth."

"My vision was blurred. There could have been a bulldog there, and I wouldn't have seen it. Anyway, what were you doing up after midnight, fully dressed and ready to go out?"

"What I told you. I needed some air."

"Sure."

"Well, what about the next morning?"

"What about it?"

"The suitcase. If it had been there, you'd have practically tripped over it."

"I can see you now putting everything back into the drawers in the early hours of the morning, with your tail between your legs. Nives, I repeat, I'm really sorry."

"No problem."

"This is a nightmare."

"Dear, take your wife's words and brand them onto your forehead. This is just the beginning."

"Wait a minute. You believe this crazy woman and not me? Okay, the donkey kick I had a hundred years ago was true . . . but all the rest? It was pretty obvious: I was letting her blather on. That's what experts advise for patients in psychiatric wards."

"Loriano, you're really the worst."

"Nives, my friend. Let him speak. He's flapping around like a pheasant in the undergrowth. He wanted the moon and now he's trapped in a snare of his own making. He's ready to swear that it's raining from the ground up."

"To tell you the truth, I'm feeling dizzy."

"I'm sorry, Nives. Are you feeling okay? Hearts at our age shouldn't skip too many beats; it's not pleasant."

"You're worrying about her? What about me?"

"Animals like you have strong blood. Just look at the effect the drops have on you, with everything you throw down your gullet."

"Drops? What drops?"

"It's not pleasant to watch your husband drink himself to death. Being a sensible wife, I make things easier for you."

"What do you mean?"

"Two tablespoons of tranquillizer."

"What?"

"The one they prescribed me when I had palpitations a lifetime ago. I pour two big spoonfuls into the flask that I put on the table every evening."

"Are you stupid, or what? A man may never wake up from a dose like that."

"God willing . . ."

"Donatella, are you saying you drug me every evening with a sleeping draught?"

"Well, at least you're not drinking two whole bottles that way. They cost money, you know. You hardly make it to the second glass. The evening news theme tune comes on, and you're ready to lie down in your sarcophagus. You can barely drag yourself into the bedroom."

"How long has this been going on?"

"I don't know. Forever."

"Forever?"

"Since the day I made it my business to stop you poisoning your liver like a halfwit."

"That stuff is addictive."

"In the meantime, you've avoided crashing into a bottomless pit."

"So that's why I have the jitters . . . ?"

"What jitters, my love?"

"You know, when I wake up in the morning with my head like a brick, and it gets worse through the day. I get into the car as heavily as if I had a sack of cement tied to each foot. Sometimes, I move my eyes and there's a delay before I see things. It makes me feel sea-sick. I only begin to feel better after two coffees and my first grappa at Momo's."

"And that's how you start your day!"

"You don't get it."

"Yes, I do. You're a drunk. But everyone knows that."

"If I stopped, I would go crazy."

"Sillari came back to life when he stopped."

"I mean the drops. If I stop taking them suddenly after years and years, my entire universe will be turned around."

"A little like what's just happened to me this evening."

"Oh God, I feel terrible already . . ."

"Listen to your wife's words. This is just the beginning."

"Oh no! I can't breathe . . ."

"And yet, until ten minutes ago, our Loriano was feeling as strong as a bull."

"Nives, fuck off."

"Dear, don't pay attention to him."

"You see what he's like? I say I'm feeling dizzy, and he goes and grabs the stage. He's such a drama queen."

"Has your head stopped spinning? Are you feeling better?"

"I feel like I'm in a dream, Donatella."

"You're telling me."

"In the sense that something's happening to me. If I tell you, you won't believe me."

"I'm all ears."

"I don't know. Maybe I have gone crazy, after all . . . I'm feeling good."

"You're feeling good?"

"Like I've never felt before. I feel as light as when I was a girl, with no troubles and no cares."

"Lucky you."

"Everything has magically melted away. Should I be worried?"

"My friend, I know what it is."

"What?"

"You've seen what Loriano is made of, and it has disgusted you. Your whole life you've been hooked on the notion of an idealized love, and then, in one phone call, you realize you've missed nothing."

"I almost feel like crying . . . Is this what being normal is like?"

"You've let go of the deadweight. Which is what I'm going to do now, quick as a flash."

"There's no way I'm going to give Laura that letter! I don't want *my* daughter to feel she has anything to do with Bottai's blood."

"Good for you."

"If only you could see me now, Donatella. I'm crying and laughing at the same time! Who would ever have imagined? All of a sudden, I feel as though I've never made any mistakes. If my knees weren't done in, I'd start dancing. And listen to this. My image of Anteo, that poor husband of mine who's never let me want for anything: suddenly, he feels like a saint. I wish he were here now! Even those two blond grandchildren whose names I can't pronounce feel like a great gift."

"Because they are."

"And this farm here, so full of memories. Donatella, it's all beautiful! Do you know what I hope now, in the midst of all this happiness? I hope God looks down on me and calls me up to him, now that I'm so full of light! Does asking to die sound reasonable to you?"

"Nobody's stopping you."

"And you, Loriano! Poor little playboy without an ounce of courage. Suddenly, I feel pity for you. I was just a bit of fun in the bushes for you. Who could resist a girl who's head-over-heels in love with you, to the point that she's ready to give herself to you entirely and wreck a marriage? You never chose me, not even for a second. And yet, there you were at our meeting place every time. Spineless little man that you are, you were content with taking home your trophy. As long as you could get your hands on me, you were prepared to make solemn promises, without giving a hoot about the fact that I was hanging on your every word. If you'd only had the vaguest idea of how much love I was ready to give you! Of how our encounters meant little or nothing to me, because I wanted all of you. I would've cut my veins to wake up in the morning, find you in my bed, and say, 'Good morning, my love.' But no. For you, I was a pastime. A plaything you could badmouth to your drinking pals, calling me an idiot and poor Anteo a certified cuckold, only to shake his hand the next minute. What hell you put me through, Loriano. And what an idiot I was! The same idiot that devoted almost half a century to your memory. Now you're there in the hall, nailed to the phone. On one side, there's the woman you disappointed; on the other, the woman you deceived. I can just see you, in your underpants, your hair uncombed, bloated with wine, shocked by the picture we have painted of you. Like in a mirror that reflects things exactly as they are, but in reverse: you're the one who's been squandered; I'm the one who's been saved. Tell me this news isn't a blessing . . . I may not have been a champion, first as a wife and then as a mother, but all of a sudden, I can shout this out to the world, now, with the clock striking the early hours of the morning: I've never deceived myself. Day after day, I've been here, gazing at the shards of my broken dreams through misty eyes. There was Laura, and Anteo, and the farm. The humble life of hard-working folk, who care about the little things: Christmas, Easter, birthdays, summer evenings . . . I was the center of this world; even more, I was the queen. But I didn't pay it any heed, because I was waging another war. Now that I realize I only gave them half of myself, I want to kick myself. And yet, there's something that warms me from head to toe: knowing that I've received a great deal and that it's all here around me and in my memories. Six lives wouldn't be long enough to leaf through the golden album that has suddenly opened inside me. I realize I've been a fool when I go back and look at the torment I actively cultivated when I was a girl, and later, when I threw away my womanhood. All the while, I was attended to in the most beautiful place in the world, and I didn't even notice. So, dear Loriano, I have you to thank. If I hadn't bled myself dry here for you this evening, I wouldn't have reaped the benefits; I wouldn't have seen Poggio Corbello as a cathedral. I thank Rosa, and the others, who decided to take possession of a hen this evening and obliged me to dial a certain number, given the emergency. Tomorrow morning, I'll withdraw half of my pension and send a gift to my grandchildren on the other side of the Alps that will make their eyes shine. Because in the end it has actually happened: I've gone crazy. With happiness."

" . . ."

"Nives, what beautiful words."

"Dear Donatella, I'm so sorry. Maybe I'm taking everything away from you. Please know it was not my intention."

"What can I say? I lived with a serenity that was never mine. It's good that the chickens have come home to roost."

"Okay, it's late now. Ciao." The widow hung up, just like that, without waiting for an answer.

Nives looked at the telephone for a minute longer. After passing the receiver from one hand to the other for so long, her arms ached and her ears were burning; the buzz reminded her of the slaps she would receive as a girl, when she'd done something naughty. More than anything else, though, a peculiar sensation ran through her body: her heart was beating strangely hard, pumping with the kind of euphoria that expert bank robbers must feel when they clutch the haul of the century to their chests as they make their escape. Then she moved, and even that was an odd feeling. Her steps felt purposeful and precise. She realized she was hungry.

Giacomina strutted under her skirt, as if she were off to do the shopping. It was a rare thing to see a mother hen so alert at that time of night. She watched the bird struggling with her chewed-off claw and felt a harmony there that warmed her heart.

The light was still on in the living room. Nives was tempted to do what poor Anteo used to do once a year, when he took it into his head to open the box and smoke a cigar. It was only when he fancied it; never for a special occasion . . . Drawing closer to the armchair, she saw the dent in the cushion where the hen had sat, hypnotized, for so long. The widow started. "Look at that!" she said out loud. "She's laid an egg."

Her first thought was that she'd fry it, sunny side up.

## ABOUT THE AUTHOR

Sacha Naspini was born in 1976 in Grosseto, a town in southern Tuscany. He has worked as an editor, art director, and screenwriter, and is the author of numerous novels and short stories which have been translated into several languages. *Nives* is his first novel to appear in English.